Ashes and Roses

The Orion Dynasty Book 5

CK Franco

Blurbs

He's the phantom billionaire no one dares touch.
I was never supposed to catch his eye.

Silas Carver rules the media world from the shadows—untouchable, ruthless, feared. Hana Brooks is a survivor just trying to keep her world intact. But when their lives collide, desire blooms from the ashes.

Secrets, scars, and enemies close in, forcing them to choose: trust the danger between them, or let it destroy everything.

Mysterious recluse. Forbidden attraction. A dark love story written in ashes and roses.

For those who have ever loved in silence, carried their scars in the shadows, and feared that trust was too fragile to hold. This story is yours. May you find the courage to believe that from ashes, roses can still bloom.

"Love is not the absence of darkness, but the courage to let another see it—and stay."

Prologue

The Phantom in the Glass

Silas Carver stood before the floor-to-ceiling windows of his penthouse, the New York skyline glittering like a thousand lies reflected in glass. To the world, he was untouchable—the strategist, the phantom tycoon, the man no one truly saw.

But tonight, the mask weighed heavier than usual.
The roses on his desk—black, edged in crimson—were more than flowers. They were memory. They were grief. They were promises he swore he would never make again.

And then he saw her.

Through the reflections of the glass, in the dim light of a crowded café below, Hana Brooks fought back against a man who thought he could belittle her. Her eyes sparked with fire, defiance wrapped in vulnerability. In that moment, Silas felt something shift—something he had buried years ago, something dangerous.

He told himself it was nothing. Just curiosity. Just another story waiting to be written.

But even as he turned away, he knew the truth.

This woman—this stranger with fire in her eyes—was about to ruin him.

Contents

The Phantom Tycoon

Hana Brooks moves through the evening's golden glow like a blade hidden in silk. The main dining room at Marigny is a hall of illusions—high ceilings stretch overhead, chandeliers shedding light too soft to reveal any truth, pooling gold across the crisp white tablecloths. Wealth hangs in the air alongside the scent of truffle oil and charred filet. Around her, a blur of designer suits and laughter echoes against marble floors. The city's elite, insulated by old money and thirteen-dollar martinis, treat the world beyond this sanctuary as rumor.

She balances a tray—crystal glasses shivering with the memory of cold—winding between men and women draped in silk and expectation. A brittle-lipped maître d' floats past, his smile as polished as the silver. Hana catches her reflection rippling in a spoon and then glances up at the clock staked high above the kitchen door, its hands marching toward the late dinner hour. She lets the clangor of voices and cutlery slide off her skin. Her jaw aches from holding a smile for strangers whose names drift in and out, as fleeting as the coats left at reception.

Table fourteen. She steadies herself, letting her hand brush the linen—soft, ironed, carrying a trace of starch and bleach beneath the pepper of tonight's amuse-bouche. The banker slouched there hasn't left his suit jacket back at the office. His hair is trimmed, and his nails are clean, each gesture slow as a coronation.

He waits until she sets a glass in front of him. "You know," he drawls, loud enough for the table beside him to hear, "your English is pretty good. Didn't expect that in a place like this."

His friends shift, eyes darting. The banker's wedding ring flashes as he flicks invisible lint from his cuff, a smirk blooming.

She does not grant him a win. She squares her shoulders and meets his gaze head-on, her voice calm and steel-bright. "Respect is always on the menu. If you can't order that, I'll find someone who will."

A beat of silence. Utensils freeze, a glacier in mid-melt.

His friends give up nervous chuckles, their laughter thin and un-sure. The banker shrugs, already looking for the next target, but she sees the flicker of embarrassment—a bloom of red at the corners of his ears. Hana's palms prickle with memory: her mother teaching her the sharpness of language; a landlord's sneer; another boss's oily smile. She presses her lips together, keeping the old hurt tucked between her ribs. Not tonight.

She clears their empties, hands steady, gathering glass and crockery as if she were building the walls she needs to get through the shift. She ignores the man's intentionally dismissive glance, her own features closed tight against any flash of pain.

"Need a higher tip to buy some manners?" the banker mutters, barely above a whisper.

She pauses, eyes on the glass in her hand. "I don't take payment for losing my spine," she says softly, not for him but for herself—and perhaps for any ghosts listening in.

She pivots away, letting the mask of professionalism settle back over her as she moves to the next table.

Across the room, in a booth where the chandelier's glow can't quite reach, Silas Carver sits in charcoal and shadow. Tonight, the city's most reclusive media king is invisible to nearly everyone—an utter contrast to the careless theater unfolding three tables away. His silver cufflinks glint, catching a shard of stray light. His phone lies dark and abandoned on the table, but his eyes track every movement at table fourteen, precise and unyielding as an astronomer mapping stars.

Silas's expression betrays nothing. There are no tells—no tightening at the jaw, no flicker across those almost-colorless eyes—but inside, calculations twist with something older and more dangerous. He's witnessed a thousand public humiliations in rooms like this, the way power bends language and rules. But Hana's retort, the stubborn steadiness at her core, interests him more than the spectacle of entitlement. He catalogs the tilt of her chin, the fire carefully hidden under her workaday grace. In a world where everyone chooses their mask, her refusal to wear his kind of armor stands out.

He sees the pain in her controlled movements—not the kind that scalds, but the quiet ache earned over years of being overlooked, misjudged, or categorized by an accent or a face. She is neither soft nor brittle. Silas's lips almost twitch. It's rare to find someone who won't barter their dignity for a larger tip, rarer still when that defiance comes wrapped in humility.

The banker stares at his empty wine glass, no longer smirking. Hana lifts her tray, exhaling, her breath shivering out along her shoulders. She rolls her neck slowly, as if willing the confrontation to slide off her, but the tension remains knotted at her temples. At another table, a woman remarks on the day's headlines, a fleeting reference to Victor Kane's latest media merger—some Manhattan predator always climbing over someone else. Hana wonders what it's like to always have the power to speak first, to never watch your words be weighed, dissected, or discarded.

A server, arms full of plates, nearly collides with Hana by the kitchen pass. Their elbows brush. The woman's voice drops low.

"Told you he was slime. You okay?"

"Seen worse," Hana says, her voice light, practiced, almost convincing. "But my patience might be the rarest thing here tonight."

The server grins. "Charge extra for it."

Hana's smile flickers, small and real. "If only I could."

She disappears into the sea of white and silver, the ambient chatter sealing around her like a force field. Silas, from his vantage in the corner, never looks away even as the noise of Manhattan's chosen rises and the rich keep feasting on whatever—or whoever—they please.

Hana steps back from the banker's table, tight-lipped and fierce, the echo of laughter and the shimmer of crystal flutes ringing through Marigny's golden-lit dusk. The white tablecloths glow like pale moons in the glamour of the dining room, each constellation of Manhattan's elite orbiting its own narrative—bankers, attorneys, a flash of designer silk trailing across the marble aisle. The room swells with voices, polished toasts layered over the distant pulse of jazz from the bar. Hana hugs her order pad to her chest, fingers pressing a shallow dent into its cardboard edge, chasing the certainty of routine over the spike of adrenaline that prickles through her veins. She sidesteps a busboy carrying a tray of oysters, her breath catching on the briny scent and the reluctant clatter of shells.

Her eyes flicker upward, searching for her manager's familiar silhouette—a lifeline, a witness, or simply a shield against the fallout of yet another rich man's cruelty. Only her manager isn't in sight. Instead, something stops her short; heat slides over her skin, neither threatening nor benign. She finds the source: across the dining room and settled into the velvet gloom of a corner booth, a man watches her with a quiet that feels almost planetary. He's a silhouette carved from shadow and purpose—charcoal suit, silver cufflinks gleaming at his wrist, angular as cathedral spires.

His eyes—unmistakably grey, metallic in the gold haze—catch hers. He does not glance away. The motion of Marigny bleeds out between them, and for a moment the whole world is narrowed to the space of a single gaze: unwavering, almost impossible in its steadiness, as if the current of the city swirls around him without ever finding purchase.

Hana's lungs thrum. She knows—on a level so deep it brushes bone—that this isn't the idle interest of another Wall Street regular who expects to be adored. There's an intelligence in the man's stillness, a calculation, yet something else smolders in the lines of his mouth, like ash swept over velvet. She can feel her pulse tighten at her throat, the bite of anxiety threading old memories beneath her ribs. Every instinct screams for her to look away, to disappear back into the world of steam and kitchen orders and safety found in ignorance. But his stare is a question—one she cannot easily ignore.

Their connection snaps taut, precarious as a glass balancing on the verge of shattering. Broken, unfinished, thrilling in a way that makes Hana's hands tremble against the order pad for just a second too long.

"Excuse me, can I get another napkin, please?"

Hana blinks, torn back by the voice of a woman at table eight, her voice candy-sweet and pointed. She manages a nod, suddenly embarrassed by her own stillness, and turns away from the stranger in the corner, but not before she notes the faint quirk at the edge of his mouth—an invitation, a challenge, or simply a reflection of her own defiance.

She moves through the shifting maze of bodies, each footstep measured. Her cheeks burn, the air in Marigny thick with perfume and ambition. The world resumes its rotations. A waiter brushes past with a pitcher of water, splashing droplets over her shoes, but Hana barely feels the chill seep in. There's only the afterimage of his grey gaze, the odd magnetism that still hooks into her gut.

She doesn't dare look back.

Inside, panic jostles with something sharper, a strange excitement stalking the shadows of her mind. She's spent years hiding, collecting herself into corners and narrow silences, always wary of being seen too clearly by those who never look beyond the surface. Now, exposed under that gaze, she feels raw and unsettled, as if every secret she's sewn inside her skin might be visible—each rough edge, every old scar. It's a sensation she can't stand, and yet she's not certain if it's fear that sets her moving so quickly or the wild, heady knowledge that she's finally been noticed by someone who sees past her practiced smile.

Hana pushes the swinging doors aside hard enough for the metal to rattle. The kitchen's heat smacks her, frying oil and rosemary, chopping knives and curses in three languages. She enters the staff hallway, breath coming shallow, her heart drumming a frantic rhythm in her throat.

"What happened out there? You look like you saw a ghost."

A voice from her left—Marcos, wearing flour on his apron and amusement in his eyes.

"Nothing. Just... someone staring. Like I was on the menu," Hana murmurs, trying for a flippant note that rings a little too thin.

"That's Manhattan," Marcos says, shrugging. "Salty old men, hungry ghosts, and bankers who think tips buy them anything."

She shoots him a wan smile, grateful for the cover, then leans against the cold tile wall, pressing her spine flat and willing her pulse to calm. The world beyond the kitchen narrows to memory—a pair of eyes that dissected her shields in a heartbeat. She swallows, promising herself that it's nothing. Just a look. Just a man. Just another Tuesday night in a city crawling with predators and ghosts alike.

Yet, when she glances back through the porthole window, seeking out the booth, she finds the seat empty. The air thrums as if something inevitable has begun, spinning outside her control.

The kitchen door swings shut behind her, leaving the world—and the man with storm-gray eyes—on the other side, watching the spot where she's vanished.

The crystal glow of Marigny's chandeliers bathes the room in honeyed light, but in the farthest corner, where velvet shadows pool, Silas Carver sits shrouded in a private dusk. The white linen hush of the dining room has grown mellow with the dinner hour—clinking glassware softens, laughter turns introspective. Silas flicks his thumb over the edge of his phone, the screen dark, his mind elsewhere. He lowers his gaze, eyes sweeping the emptiness Hana Brooks left in her wake. For a moment, it is as if the air itself mourns her absence; voices drift around him, unheeded.

He releases a measured breath and lets the mask of indifference settle over his features—a rare art, mastered over years spent fencing with

Manhattan's titans. The restaurant's warmth can't quite cut through the steel in his bones. Across the room, golden lamps make ghosts of faces—bankers, patrons, their power lacquered over with expensive scent and easy scorn—but none of them hold his attention.

Silas's mind replays Hana's defiant words, the flint-strike of her tone ringing louder than the dull chorus of cutlery. He pictures the set of her jaw, the blaze that dared that banker to look at her like she was furniture. *She is not small, not to be dismissed.* But then—he'd seen it—the waver behind her eyes, swift as a shadow underwater. That flicker is what haunts him. He's spent years deciphering double-speak, decoding the calculus of power, but here was something truer—so raw it made him restless.

He pictures her again: slender, braced for impact, drawn taut by invisible strings—pride, pain, something unnamed. It's rare to see that blend: unbreakable spirit stitched together with wounds not yet calloused. It calls to him in ways that unsettle his well-fortified calm. He leans back, knuckles white against the cool glass, letting silence seep into the hollows inside him. What would it cost to take someone like that, bring her in from the cold—into *his* shadows?

A passing server snaps him back to the room; the faint bite of freshly ground black pepper hangs in the air. Somewhere, red wine blooms into a glass, and a woman's laugh cracks like glass over stone. Silas barely hears. He weighs, with his strategist's mind, the thousand angles—assets, vulnerabilities. Hana is unpredictable, that much is now fact. In his world, unpredictability is a liability; a single exposed nerve can unravel a decade of secrets. Yet, the memory of her spine straightening under insult makes him hunger for more.

He finds himself tracing possibilities, building and discarding futures in the vault of his mind. Hana, given a taste of his world—would she bow, or would she flare bright and burn herself out against it?

Would she be an ally, a threat, or something neither could account for? If she is noticed by Victor Kane, that wolf prowling at the city's gate, or by Selena Voss and her razor ambitions, Hana could become collateral—broken for having brushed his orbit. He feels suddenly the echo of old grief—a mother lost, a legacy bruised by trust misplaced. His caution is a skin he cannot shed.

Yet underneath it all, an urge coils—irrational, insistent. The Brotherhood's code: guard at all costs. The secret that, if breached, would not only raze his own life but the lives of all sworn to him. Hana's fire is dangerous. And yet it's precisely that danger that compels—the flicker of something honest in a world of artifice. He wonders, not for the first time, if the life he's built isn't a fortress but a cage.

He signals for the check, the gesture almost invisible. The maître d', quick and discreet, glides to his table, no words exchanged beyond a tight nod, but Silas catches the subtlest flick of eyes—curiosity, suspicion maybe. He returns nothing. Phantom, predator. Still, inside, the plan begins to take shape: a chance opportunity, tailored so she believes she's stumbled into fortune rather than design. It's always better if they choose the trap themselves.

A voice interrupts his brooding, just as the bill is presented.

"Is everything to your liking this evening, Mr. Carver?"

Silas doesn't look directly at the host. "Impeccable, as always. Send my compliments to the kitchen."

A pause.

"We do hope we'll see you again soon. You find our staff... satisfactory, I trust?"

Silas's lips curve with an irony the host will never parse. "More than satisfactory. Exceptional."

He rises, smooth and unhurried. The evening chill bleeds in through the foyer's glass, spiced with roasting chestnuts from a cart outside, the city's roar pressing faintly through insulated stone. He glances, just once, toward the staff hallway—where the ghost of Hana's resistance still seems to linger, a ripple through the air. The risk, the draw, and the danger—all braided tightly now in his chest. He allows the barest smile, unreadable, born not of triumph but of anticipation. Then he's gone, melting into Manhattan's incandescent night, plotting the first gentle snare that will beckon Hana out of her shadows and into his.

The Invitation

A rain mist peels down the Manhattan glass, softening the city's sharp, bladed skyline. Silas Carver's office, perched high above the wet hum of traffic, is silent, save for the low murmur of string music thrumming from hidden speakers. He stands behind his obsidian desk, pale light feathering the faint scar along his jaw. His gaze is distant, calculating. When his assistant enters—silent, efficient—Silas arches a brow, slides a single cream envelope forward, and speaks with a voice both smooth and edged.

"This letter. Hana Brooks. Discretion, always. And make sure it's delivered at close." His words are not a request but a mandate, the kind that leaves no argument blooming in the dusty air. The assistant pockets the envelope and treads from the sanctum, boots never echoing, as if wary of waking something ancient.

Down below, the old café at the corner sags against the day. Hana Brooks moves with the practiced economy of a survivor—the scrape of plates, the crunch of broken biscotti underfoot, the roasted dark of espresso lacing the air. Her uniform apron chafes against her hips;

sweat sticks her hair to her nape. At table six, a man complains that his coffee is "scorched," eyes flicking from her scar to her hands as if counting her worth in invisible ink. She swallows her retort, gives him a brittle smile, and fetches a refill, steps clipped. Her body aches in places her heart can't even name.

At shift's end, while the city outside steams with fading sunlight, she bundles tip coins into her palm, her thumb aching from hours of work. There—on top of the receipts—a neat cream envelope stares up at her. Her name, inked in elegant black: Hana Brooks. It's the sort of stationery that belongs in the hands of trust-fund kids, not in the grease-stained aftermath of a Greenwich café. For a moment, her throat closes around her own name, violent and silent.

She turns the envelope over, fingers the edge, her heart banging out a fragile panic. Someone is watching, a voice murmurs. Someone who knows how to find you, no matter how small you make yourself. She feels the burn of old humiliations, credit denials, the overhaul of her life after the fallout with him—her ex whose shadow still lingers in every unanswered call and unpaid bill. She shoves the envelope into her apron, the paper cool against her damp skin.

The next hour crawls. Lights dim. The mosaic behind the counter flickers blue and gold, casting the ghost of other people's dreams on the walls. Hana hauls a bucket across the floor, her thoughts whirring like moths on a dying bulb. What if it's a scam? A threat? Another debt disguised as a gift? But what if, this time, it's real? Her mind conjures strange futures: herself behind an editorial desk, sleeves rolled back, papers fluttering like the wings of a new life. She imagines a salary that erases the weight of every creditor's threat, imagines walking into a grocery store without fear tugging at her ribs. A spiraling hope uncoils, alien and bright, tangled with suspicion.

But she knows what promises cost. How easily hope can tip into hunger and shame. After all, the world she scrapes by in isn't ruled by fairy tales, but by men like Silas Carver—whose power slices through a city like glass. Victor Kane's face flashes to mind from TV headlines—the ruthless rival, always circling, always plotting, proof that powerful people use pawns and leave them broken.

Hana scrubs the sink until suds sting her cuticles. Still, the envelope waits. She stares at the name—her name—as if it might rearrange itself in the soft puddle of fluorescent light.

She steps outside, breath raw against the thick syrup of rain. The hum of neon signs—bakery, tattoo shop, newsagent—grows distant as she ducks into the alley. Only the soft, stubborn heartbeat of the city remains, rain quietly drumming on rubbish bins, the scent of hot concrete and spent cigarettes thick in the air.

Her hands shake as she tears open the envelope. The paper inside is heavy, embossed, perfumed faintly with something metallic—unnervingly expensive. She reads: Orion Media Group offers her a junior editor position. Salary, start date, signature line. The words spin, skewering her to the brick wall behind her. The letter might as well be written by the Devil: temptation wrapped in gold leaf, every syllable soaked in shadow. She swallows, her mouth dry.

She pulls out her phone and stabs in the number. There's a pause—someone picks up, professional, brisk: "Orion Group, this is Ms. Lee." Hana's voice emerges small but fierce.

"This is Hana Brooks. I—" she hesitates, eyes squeezed shut "—I'm calling to accept the interview. Monday, right?" The rhythm of her voice conjures a confidence she doesn't own.

"Yes, Ms. Brooks. We'll expect you at nine. Welcome to Orion."

She ends the call, chin tucked, breath trembling. Behind the plate-glass window, Silas watches—barely a flicker of his lips betrays satisfaction, eyes gone sharp as a knife's tip. Stormlight crawls over his reflection, blurring the lines between watcher and watched.

Alone in the alley, Hana stares at the city's trembling horizon—sunset bleeding gold into the blue, skyscrapers lit like the promise of another world. She presses her fists to her eyes. Dread and impossible hope spiral, tangled. She steps forward, the weight of the offer burning in her pocket, as Manhattan's lamps stutter awake against the coming dark.

The city crowds part enough for Hana Brooks to find her place on the icy sidewalk, boots planted between gusts of wind and constellation-bright cigarette ends. Her gaze sweeps up the glass-and-chrome monolith of Orion Media Group. Manhattan's reflection shimmers in sharp, fractured lines across the skyscraper's surface. Her fists clench inside her jacket pockets, each breath thin in her chest, steadying her against the skyscraper's inhuman, glacial symmetry. The revolving doors spin endlessly, swallowing and spilling out men and women in knife-edge coats and bright, impassive shoes—none of them look back.

Inside the lobby, everything is polished marble and chrome so clean it feels surgical. The hush is so complete that Hana can hear the faint scuff of her own soles echoing over the tiles. For a moment, she catches her battered reflection in the smoked glass panel by the security desk: hair too dark and wild, worry-shadowed eyes, the old crescent scar above her brow. She smooths her sleeve, chin up. She's survived worse. She will not let her hands shake.

A woman in a colorless suit—every edge sharp as the city skyline—waits by the front desk. "Ms. Brooks?" The woman's voice is precise as a scalpel. "Right this way." She leads Hana without a word through corridors lined with glass-walled boardrooms, the ceilings so high they swallow sound. Each step drills deeper into the heart of the empire, past screens that flicker with world news, market graphs, and surreal moving headlines. Employees barely glance up. When they do, their eyes register, assess, dismiss. The unspoken verdict: one more contender in a city built on rivals.

They pass a clutch of men in bespoke suits whose laughter crackles too loud, brittle and jagged as ice. One nods to the HR manager, but his eyes flick to Hana and slide away, uncurious, already recataloguing her as risk or irrelevance. At a glass doorway, the woman pauses and gestures for Hana to enter a smaller chamber with wall-to-wall screens. A junior assistant—barely older than Hana but already cultivated into corporate anonymity—waits behind a pristine desk, head bowed over a sleek, glowing tablet.

"Your orientation materials are loaded here." She hands Hana a polyester badge, crisp and cold as a new blade. "Scan for access everywhere except executive floors. Lunch is thirty minutes. Passwords autogenerate. Please be discreet with confidential documents." Her voice barely meets Hana's gaze, eyes skimming just past her shoulder. Rules are recited, perfectly memorized, not one wasted syllable.

The air tastes faintly of ozone and the distant, metallic perfume of artificial lilies. Hana's fingers close around the badge. The light weight belies the heft of expectation. She swallows, blinking as a notification pings on one of the distant tablets—words scrolling in silent code. This is not a place of second chances.

Through seamless walls, the golden-lit mezzanine glows—high above, a dark figure stands between drifting department heads. Silas Carver: silver-threaded hair, black suit, back turned to the world he commands. He tilts his head in profile, never looking down; yet as the HR manager's hand flicks toward Hana, she catches—there, a glimmer of movement. Like a predator that knows every pulse in its den. The glass pretends anonymity, but power sweeps beneath the surface, watchful, predatory, precise.

She's led to a cubicle, half-submerged in a tide of murmuring editors. The hum of the bullpen rises and dips through the air, alive with urgency and sharp, synthetic light. Hana slides into a chair warmed by another's body heat, logs in as directed, her heart thudding in her throat. On the far side of the divider, a woman with platinum nails whispers, "That's the new one, right?"

"I heard Carver's got plans for her. Wonder if she'll last the month."

"She's under review first."

Someone snorts. "They *all* are."

Hana pretends to type. The screen glows, the dashboard blinks up deadlines: six articles, three briefings, two research packets. A cascade of requests, each flagged urgent, each tagged to names she recognizes from headlines. A message pings from an editor: Please revise—tone inappropriate for our brand.

Her hands hover above the keyboard. She smells the synthetic tang of floor wax and overheated hardware. Her stomach knots, a hollow pang twisting through adrenaline and dread.

A rival staffer circles. "Need help?" The faux warmth in the woman's smile is cut glass. "Newbies always have trouble finding their groove."

Hana meets her eyes. "I'll manage."

A shrug; the woman glides away.

Her nerves snap tight, then coil. This world is lined with elegant traps—a misplaced word, a tone, a look. Around her, the orchestra of clacking keys, the occasional hiss of the espresso machine by the break room. Her pulse beats loud in her ears, in time with the digital clock, every second a test.

She's survived colder places. The streets taught her what it meant to be invisible one moment, a target the next. She learned, years ago, to keep her head down, to read every slight, to let wounds grow callous. The system here is more polished, the predators dressed in silk instead of steel, but the hunger's the same. The rules: spoken in looks, in who gets called to which meeting, in how close the manager stands beside your desk.

In New York's most mythic media kingdom, hierarchy is as tangible as humidity before a storm. Power moves unseen up there in the glass, where men like Silas Carver orchestrate fates without stepping into the fray.

She can feel the gaze from above, even if the man himself never turns. Victor Kane, Selena Voss—names from whispered warnings about rival executives who would devour the weak and ambitious alike—exist somewhere, waiting to pounce once you trip.

Hana closes her fingers around her badge. The plastic bites her palm. She lets the tension simmer, lets her chest fill with something molten and sharp. She will not break, not here, not with New York watching and wolves circling.

Behind her, voices fade to static, but the heat of hostile stares lingers, braiding into the uneasy promise that she's now inside the empire's gates—alone, but unbowed.

Hana threads her way through the glass-veined labyrinth of the Orion Media Group. The corridor walls shimmer with a silvery chill, modern art blooming in jagged reds and blacks behind tempered glass. The elevator's hush swallows the scuff of her shoes. The overhead lights cast shadows that move like liquid, and every face she passes in those first minutes—every zeroed-in gaze, every clipped nod—seems cataloged and filed for later.

At her first editorial meeting, she introduces herself: "Hana Brooks, junior editor." The words feel borrowed, not lived-in. A row of faces lifts. Some bored, some appraising, not a lick of warmth beneath the polite murmurs. She sits, feeling the scrape of a metal chair against marble, and registers the undercurrents—how a young woman named Elara glances at another, then folds her arms with intent, how a silver-haired copy chief makes reference to a "Brotherhood assignment" without ever explaining it. Details flicker: the men and women who speak as if sharing a language she's not supposed to understand. She notes their camaraderie, the shorthand and sharp silences. She doesn't ask.

The meeting bleeds into another. Hana speaks when pressed, keeps her answers short. She recognizes the power in being underestimated—a skill first honed flicking wet mugs at drunk customers, then tested under the fluorescent lights and gnawing debt at her last apartment. Here, the air buzzes with a different kind of threat: not fists or raised voices, but secrets. And power, measured in what is said and what is not.

By mid-morning, she slides into the break room, the acrid smell of burned coffee stinging her nose, the grease of a donut box sticky under her palm. The hum of the copier masks a conversation behind stacks of files. Two voices—one clipped and nasal, the other oily with nerves—dance just out of sight.

"Have you heard from Caius's team?" the department head asks, voice spiked with worry.

"Mmm. They're lawyering up. Blackwell's handling it personally. Rumor is, Darius gave notice to Lucien late last night." The senior reporter's glance shaves the edge of panic. "Victor Kane's circling. And that Voss woman—she's got half the Board trembling."

A nervous laugh. "If the Brotherhood falls, we're all—"

The copier clangs, paper spits out. The voices snap off, replaced by brittle laughter as Hana leaves, one more note added to her private ledger of danger. The names—Caius, Lucien, Darius—anchor her suspicions: the people who rule this empire play a game well beyond her debt-riddled, bruised horizon. Victor Kane. Selena Voss. Antagonists outside the glass, it seems, are real enough to have nerves shaken and meetings halted.

She returns to her tasks, shoulders prickling with caution, words swirling in her head alongside her own tangle of worries.

A senior editor intercepts her in the hall. Sleek suit, sharp eyes that could slice meat. The smile barely touches his mouth.

"You're Hana, right? Fresh blood." His tone is soft as refrigeration. "Little advice. This place spits out those who don't pay attention—especially outsiders. You keep your head down. Eyes open. Or you'll wish you'd left with your last paycheck."

He doesn't wait for her answer, but she lets her chin lift ever so slightly. "Thanks for the warning," she says, keeping her voice as cool as his, remembering every bar mat she ever wrung out with shaking hands, every landlord who threatened to change locks if the rent ran another day late.

Lunch lasts ten minutes, just enough time to taste the city's tension through the glass. The skyline pulses with metallic glare. Hana chews her sandwich, fingers cold, jaw set, the rhythm of her breath measured and silent.

Around two, her desk phone blinks. A PA summons her to a small, fishbowl office. The city glowers beyond the glass walls. She sits, hands folded, knees pressed together. Then the phone rings. Silence for a single breath—then Silas Carver's voice, low and unyielding, each word weighed like gold coins.

"Miss Brooks. I trust your first day is proving... enlightening."

She tastes metal, sharp on her tongue, and says, "It's certainly something."

"There are many layers to Orion," he continues, his voice steady as rainfall on glass. "You've stepped into a world where loyalty is both currency and curse. Remember, nothing here is what it seems." The line clicks dead, leaving her with the hush of white noise and a heart knocking too fast.

Hana leans back, letting the chair's chill settle into her spine. Through the window, Manhattan's arteries flicker to life as night encroaches, the city burning with secrets and neon lies. Beneath the marble and mirror of this place, she senses a nest of rivalries—Victor Kane in the shadows, Selena Voss weaving her own labyrinth. Names spoken in whispers, power knotted in every brittle smile. Her hands tremble, just barely, but she makes a fist around her fear.

She's survived worse. Far worse. Yet nothing in her past—no debt notice, no betrayal—quite matches the magnitude of threat she feels now. And yet, as the city unfolds beneath her, Hana does not yield. She sits taller, her gaze catching the sunset's blood on glass, resolve steeping in her chest. Ensnared in a web spun long before she arrived, she refuses to become the prey.

The Gentleman's Shadow

The chandeliers drip gold and shadow over the ballroom, casting pools of dim light that make silk shimmer and sequins flicker like tiny stars. Hana stands near the entry, her dress a river of slate gray, simple and stark among the waves of designer gowns and razor-edged suits. The scent of expensive perfume and cologne floats thick through the air, commingling with the sharpened tang of champagne. All around, laughter curls in practiced arcs; glasses clink, and the polished floors appear slick enough to swallow secrets whole.

She hugs her cheap clutch to her side, her knuckles pale against the fraying velvet. Beneath conversations about news, mergers, and art hang strands of warning too subtle for the uninitiated. There's the executive's well-timed glance at his rival—an unspoken threat delivered under the guise of a toast. There, a pair of scions in glittering heels murmur about resignations and betrayals between sips of aged Bordeaux. In this world, currency flows in trust and loyalty, traded in coded phrases and favors owed. The city's elite traffic in both fortunes and futures, every smile a chess move.

Hana knows how visible she is—knows the overhead lights catch the nervous tremble in her hands, the way she reads the room too long before entering it. Her borrowed dress is too tight across the ribs, and her heels pinch with every step. She moves through the crowd like a shadow darting across fire, determined not to flinch. But inside, her own heart batters against her composure, threatening to crack her resolve.

What would it be like to truly belong here? Maybe a different girl, forged elsewhere. Not one who counts tips and quarters at midnight or who measures her voice to keep past debts at bay. She doubts her ability to hide the hunger in her eyes—a hunger not for caviar or champagne, but for a place where no one can corner her again. Her unease feels raw, visible, like the scar above her brow that tonight's makeup can't quite erase. Maybe they all see it; maybe it's just her.

She edges along the marble perimeter, circling the base of a gilded column laced with real, blood-dark roses. The petals breathe their metallic sweetness, warning and invitation mingled in each unfurling bloom. Voices fall away as she passes, or perhaps it only seems that way. She searches for the bar, hoping a tonic or a glass of wine will steady her, but just as she steps toward her destination, a wall of navy wool and cologne materializes in her path.

The executive's smile is all teeth, all calculation. His eyes rake her from brow to shoe, cataloging her like a curious new acquisition. Perhaps she's just another rumor—one of Silas Carver's odd indulgences, an upstart with no shields and no alliances.

"Lost, aren't we?" His voice slides between the notes of conversation, soft for her but grating. "It's easy to get turned around, rookie. You know—without a guide."

She steels her shoulders and answers, "I'm finding my way just fine, thanks."

He edges closer, his shadow blending with hers beneath the flickering lights. "Funny. Most new hires earn their keep by helping someone like me. Just a whisper. A hint about Silas's next play. You'd be surprised what a little info buys in this crowd."

She swallows. The bar is just steps behind him, yet impossibly far. Hana squares her jaw, forcing herself not to shrink beneath the heat of his scrutiny. With practiced casualness, he slides an expensive drink toward her on the gilded ledge; the glass catches the red of the roses, painting her knuckles crimson.

"I don't—" she starts.

"You do," he interrupts, his voice thinning to silk-edged steel. "You owe your spot to someone's goodwill. Don't pretend you don't. Around here, that debt means something."

Inside, shame flashes hot—she's painfully aware of how quickly opportunity can become risk. Yet she refuses his net. "I don't share what isn't mine to share." Her words are quiet, but even to her own ears, they sound brittle, fragile as spun sugar.

He leans in, so close she can taste the remains of his bourbon, spiced and sour. "People think loyalty will keep them safe. But in this city, safety is just the name of a deal you haven't seen go wrong. I'd hate to see you on the wrong side."

Conversation all around doesn't slow. Two women nearby trade stories, laughter rising above the bar's glassware, pretending not to see. Somewhere, a short staccato note from a string quartet cuts through, and a server in black lingers just out of reach, attentive but unhelpful.

She doesn't back down, but her nails draw little crescents in her palm. "Then maybe you should worry less about me and more about the people you owe."

He stiffens, his stare sharpening, but whatever venom he's preparing dies unspoken as the air behind Hana tightens. In one breath, the room's temperature drops. A ripple of awareness sweeps outward from the gilded column.

Silas Carver stands at her back—silent, composed, the storm that makes the sea go still. His arrival doesn't announce itself, but people sense it: the hush on the parquet, the way heads turn discreetly. There's no anger in his body, just a coiled calm, an expectation that things will change course now that he's entered the fray.

The executive falters, half a word hanging in the air. Silas's gaze—stone-gray, unreadable—fixes on him, and all the rehearsed bravado in the room seems to evaporate. Conversations narrow to whispers as silken as the roses, and even security stirs, uncertain if they're supposed to intervene or merely bear witness.

Between the roses and the city's wolves, Hana stands very still, her pulse thudding in her ears. She recognizes now the buried rules behind the city's glitter—how a man like Silas Carver can tilt the entire axis of a room, making enemies and allies both hesitate. There are worlds within worlds here, and tonight, she is both exposed and, for one breathless moment, shielded.

Silas Carver's smile is a blade, courteous but wickedly sharp. He turns to the executive—Kane, a familiar fixture in every rumor-laden corner of Manhattan's media world—announcing his name with velvet softness that bares an edge. "Victor. I wonder—is your interest in my new colleagues always so...personal, or is tonight special?"

Victor Kane's laugh is brittle as ice underfoot. His glass rests unevenly in his hand, the amber liquor trembling in ways he does not allow his face to betray. "You recruit well, Carver. Bright-eyed, nervous—new blood always stirs talk, doesn't it? Just making sure your company's best-kept secrets aren't left in the wrong hands." His gaze darts, searching for backup, but the perimeter of chatter hushes. The gilded column's roses cast ghostly shadows across the floor, petals bleeding crimson beneath the ambient light.

Silas's tone doesn't break stride. "If anything of mine was ever at risk, Victor, I assure you, you'd be the first to know. But I hope you weren't mistaking hospitality for an interrogation. Miss Brooks is the farthest thing from careless." His gaze is steady enough to flatten rivers, his eyes cold but polite—never raising his voice, never breaking form, even as a warning smolders underneath.

Victor shifts, the grin slow to vanish, battling for some foothold of superiority. "I'd never suggest otherwise. I just think it's good for newcomers to learn how our industry works. It's a cutthroat jungle out here." His fingers blanch knuckle-white on the glass, and the laughter in his voice is thinner now, forced through clenched teeth. "We look out for our own, don't we?"

The crowd has shrunk back, their bodies angled just so—enough to turn the confrontation into theater, but no one dares join the scene. In this rare pocket of stillness, everything contracts: the air, heavy with cologne and champagne; the distant strings of a quartet muffled to a heartbeat beneath the ballroom's hum.

Silas glances at Hana, and suddenly his physical presence becomes palpable. He folds into the space between her and Victor, nudging a slim wedge of safety with his body language alone. His fingers brush Hana's lightly—just a fleeting touch at the curve of her wrist, barely more than a whisper of warmth at her pulse point—and for a beat, the world recalibrates.

Hana's breath stutters but does not escape. The fabric of her simple dress prickles with sudden awareness, the cold bite of anxiety fading beneath the phantom heat where his skin met hers. She ought to recoil—every warning stitched into her since girlhood tells her to distrust such gestures from men with power. Yet in that moment, Silas feels nothing like the wolves she's learned to sidestep in back alleys and break rooms. The way he shields her is precise, not possessive—intentional protection that says, This far, and no farther.

Inside her, something loosens—a thread pulled gently free from the tangled knot of hardened wariness. The ballroom, predatory and dazzling, momentarily recedes. She looks up, meeting the storm-gray of Silas's eyes, and in their depth finds not hunger, but something achingly human. Uncertainty and care flash there, quick as a secret apologizing for its own existence.

Victor, caught in an untenable check, hesitates. The mask slips for a blink, revealing a sliver of the fury and calculation that made his name in the city's darkest headlines. He glances around, seeking rescue, finds none. There is no ally now—not in a room made cavernous by Silas's certainty. "My apologies," Victor mutters, his eyes narrowing as he capitulates, the words falling flat and flavorless. His next breath is shallow, a vain attempt to reclaim lost dominance. Then he's gone—melted into shadows beyond the roses, his bravado abandoned among the murmurs that resume with careful, guilty vigor.

Silas's relaxed smile is a different weapon: a silent affirmation for Hana alone. In the haze of clinking ice and low voices, his posture eases, the lines at his mouth unfurling as the tension bleeds away from his shoulders. He turns to Hana, giving her a nod almost imperceptible, inviting her into the rare calm his presence affords.

Hana's hand tingles where his touch lingered. For a moment, the storybook version of Silas Carver—the untouchable titan, faceless in headlines—falls away. In his eyes, she sees the man, not the myth: composed yet weary, protective in ways rumor will never tell. She's surprised by how quickly her usual armor falters—how the lightest brush of his skin, the briefest flash of unguarded concern, wedges into the cracks of her resolve.

For as long as she can remember, gatherings like this meant being invisible or being prey. She's learned the cues: lower your eyes, keep your secrets, endure until it's safe to disappear. But tonight, under the watchful gaze of red roses and masked power, a new equation forms—one in which she might not have to face wolves alone.

A slow, creeping hope circles at the edge of her thoughts, sharp and sweet. She can't trust this, not completely. Her past is too fresh, her old scars too close to the surface. But still, she cannot deny the visceral truth of this moment: that somewhere inside the strategist's fortress, something gentle waits for her.

Silas meets her gaze and holds it. Behind him, the city's elite resume their games, but in this strip of shadow, the world has narrowed to two—strangers at the edge of a battlefield, testing what it means to believe in another's silent promise.

Silas leads Hana away from the crush of the ballroom, his hand a mere breath from the small of her back. Amber light slants through the archway ahead, flickering over the lush darkness within. They enter a lounge cocooned in midnight velvets, the air thick with the faint scent of rose oil and aged scotch. Golden sconces flicker above, swirling shadows along the walls; the music from the party dissolves into a low, distant thrum.

He pauses by a broad, marble-topped table and gestures—a silent invitation. Hana moves stiffly, clutching her bag to her chest. Her heels click, awkward and out of place on the expensive rug. The lounge feels far too elegant for her thrift-shop dress, its rough seams suddenly noticeable against her skin.

Silas settles onto a charcoal sofa, perfectly at ease. His suit molds to him like a second skin, the crisp lines immaculate. For a moment, they are silent—he, composed and unreadable; she, fidgeting, replaying the executive's sneer over and over. Her pulse is still rabbit-fast. The hush saturates the space, heavy with everything unspoken.

"Are you all right?" His voice is low, a single ripple across the velvet quiet. He pours water from a decanter, the glass clinking delicately, and slides it toward her with a gentle nudge.

She hesitates, her fingers brushing the chilled crystal. "Thank you," she says breathlessly, the word as fragile as the glass in her hand. "I wasn't... expecting that. Any of that."

Silas's gaze searches hers, unblinking and close-cutting. The lines around his eyes soften. "He shouldn't have cornered you. People like him forget basic decency behind a designer name badge."

She risks a look at him, her nerves raw. "Is it always like this? With your world?" Her fingers tremble, water threatening to spill. "I felt... outmatched. A little stupid, honestly. Like I didn't belong, like everyone could see I'm an outsider."

Silas lets the silence fall for a moment like a shroud before speaking, his eyes fixed on the melting ice in her glass. "You're not stupid, Hana. This room is full of those who learned to wear masks. Every smile has teeth behind it." His voice is barely above a whisper, threading the dark. "But being noticed here is dangerous. Sometimes I envy those who can disappear."

She studies him, searching the grooves in his face, the careful arrangement of posture and calm. There's a kind of sadness in the way he says it—a regret flickering beneath the ironclad composure. She thinks of the rumors: Silas Carver, the phantom tycoon moving unseen behind every scandal, every deal. Yet here he sits across from her, stripped of arrogance, as if he's shedding armor.

A chorus of laughter gusts in from the hallway, muffled. She glances down, tracing a drop of condensation across her palm. "Do you ever get tired? Of pretending?"

He allows a wry curve to his mouth. "It's safer, sometimes. People believe the shadows."

A pause. Only the sound of her shallow breathing fills it. Her mask feels looser, just for now, in this hush away from sharp eyes and sharper tongues. She wants to thank him again, but words flutter and die behind her teeth. Something about his steadiness, that controlled gravity, draws her in. It should frighten her, but it doesn't. Not here.

He leans forward, resting his forearms on his knees—close enough to see the faint silver at his temples, the scar at his jaw softening beneath the golden light. "You did well," he murmurs. "Most people would've let him walk all over them. You didn't."

Hana lifts her head, surprised to find her eyes stinging. For a breath, she lets herself be seen—really seen—in a way that is dangerous and oddly gentle. She tries to hold onto her walls, but they feel thinner with every heartbeat.

He straightens, giving her space. "You don't owe anyone anything, Hana. Least of all men like that."

She exhales. Something warm loosens in her chest.

"You might regret saying that." She tries for levity, but her voice cracks, too soft around the edges.

"I rarely say anything I regret," he answers, a ghost of amusement coloring his words. "I'm careful, usually."

She laughs—a small, uncertain thing—caught somewhere between gratitude and disbelief. For a long beat, neither tries to fill the silence.

She rises first, smoothing her dress, and finds him just behind her, also standing. Their eyes meet. All the slick bravado and ballroom politicking has fallen away, and what's left is a charge—a current running between two people balanced on the knife-edge of possibility.

He doesn't move to touch her. Neither does she flinch away. It's enough, the two of them suspended in this sliver of quiet, sharing the secret knowledge that outside, Victor Kane and his viperish kind are waiting, watching, always hungry for missteps.

She finally turns, stepping out of the lounge's warm light, the noise swelling to meet her. Hana does not know what she wants from Silas Carver or what it might cost. But in this moment, she's changed—barely noticeable, but irreversible, like the first crack through old ice.

Coffee and Secrets

The north elevator glides without a hum, the air cool and so precisely filtered that even the faint trace of last night's rain seems banished. Hana's reflection darts in and out of the glass, each light panel looming above as a silent audience to her own steadying breath. When the doors part, she's thrust into a world where the laws of gravity seem different: marble sprawled in wide, mirror-bright ribbons; steel and glass drawing the skyline so close that the city itself appears caged. Her heels strike a sharp, patient rhythm, every step both a challenge and a rehearsal. Silas Carver stands by the doorway of his empire's throne, tailored in a shade of midnight, his gaze as stormcloud grey as the windows behind him. He neither smiles nor frowns, simply watches—a sculptor waiting to see if his creation holds together.

She eases her voice into something just short of deferential as she greets him. "Mr. Carver."

Silas's nod is so slight it could be mistaken for a trick of the light, but his eyes narrow with a precise focus that is anything but absent. "Ms. Brooks." His hand sketches a silent invitation inside.

Hana moves—every sensation recalibrated as she crosses into his territory. The ambient hush deepens, muffled slightly by hidden speakers leaking a thread of cello and piano, sophisticated but unplaceable. His office could be a museum, every detail engineered for effect: the city's rush arranged as a backdrop, a mahogany desk broad and immaculately empty except for two small, blue-glazed cups. The scent of dark roast blooms—an edge of bitterness, cinnamon coiling above one mug as Silas's young assistant sets them down with brisk efficiency. The click of cup on wood, the muted friction of linen napkin, and then the quiet is theirs alone.

Silas gestures. "Please."

Windows wrap around the room, the ragged teeth of Manhattan displayed in morning sunlight and glass. Hana sinks into the chair opposite, letting him take in the shoes, the conservative blouse, her hair pulled back from her scar, resolute. She reaches for the cup dusted with cinnamon and allows a crooked smile.

"So this is what the seat of power looks like." Her tone threads amusement through the formality, her gaze darting behind him to the horizon. "Do you enjoy ruling from your throne?"

Something imperceptible loosens in Silas's posture. He glances outside, then folds his hands, index fingers pressed lightly together.

"Some days, it's nothing but paperwork and smoke." His answer comes in that even, clinical voice she's already begun to decode for subtext. "The view is a perk, not protection."

She suppresses a laugh, letting the silence curl expectantly. Around them, the city flickers—horns, a distant siren, the pulse of ambition so deep it nearly vibrates through her seat.

"So what exactly am I doing here, Mr. Carver?" Her fingers curve gently around the porcelain, warmth seeping up to meet her pulse. "You said it was an 'opportunity,' not—what did you call it?—'indentured servitude.' Yet the job title's still vague. Social media liaison? Digital asset analyst? I'm not an oracle, but I do like knowing what people want."

Silas's mouth contracts into a line. For a moment, he seems to be measuring the length of a shadow. "The company values versatility. Initiative. I brought you here because I'm curious what you'll do with the opportunity—if you choose to stay."

She laughs, soft but pointed. His words ripple across the desk like a forecast deliberately clouded. Hana leans forward, her elbows nearly at the table's edge. "And loyalty—how do you buy that here? Stale corporate slogans, or is there some secret handshake I missed at orientation?"

The tension in the room shifts, as if a knot behind Silas's ribcage loosens for the first time all morning. His eyebrow arches—a fleeting, involuntary tic that undermines the marble coolness.

"We don't buy loyalty, Ms. Brooks." His lips twitch, almost reluctant. Then the mask fractures: an actual, unguarded smile that illuminates the scar at his jaw. It lasts only a heartbeat but hangs between them, changing the geometry of the air.

She's caught off guard, not by the smile itself, but by the moment it exists at all—something brittle and real, unscripted in a place where everything else feels rehearsed. Reflexively, she finds herself smiling, too, and the sensation is perilous in a way she hadn't expected. The brittle tension between them softens, just a degree, as if they both sense the rules might be rewritten by accident.

This dance—half-challenge, half-invitation—reminds her of all the times she's deflected trouble with humor, the way she's learned to spar to keep the world at arm's length. But Silas's eyes search hers with a deliberateness that turns every word, every gesture, into a test.

In this glass fortress, power is measured in silences and glances. Hana feels the cold fire of ambition at her back, the brittle security of her new "opportunity" pressed against ambitions she wouldn't dare speak aloud. She recognizes something mirrored in Silas—an isolation masked by command, a curiosity careful as a blade kept sheathed. They're both performing, both watching for cracks.

Yet as his smile fades, she senses the possibility of something far more dangerous than professional acceptance—a recognition. In the flicker of vulnerability she's caught, she glimpses the real man: neither king nor phantom, but someone hunted by his own secrets in a kingdom built on glass.

Just for a heartbeat, the lines blur between threat and promise. When she glances away, Hana knows she won't be able to forget how it felt to see him, unmasked, even for that single, accidental flash. Silas studies her with the caution of a man expecting attack, or perhaps an answer. Something in the room has shifted, as if the city itself is watching and waiting to see which of them will move first.

Hana sets her cup down with deliberate care, the porcelain striking a muted note against the mahogany desk. The air is spiced with cinnamon and city ozone, sharp and cold through the plate glass. Her gaze finds Silas beyond the swirl of steam—a man built from discipline, myth, and shadows.

"Is that reputation of yours gospel?" Hana says, her voice even, shoulders squared. "Are you as ruthless as the headlines promise? Or is there a human somewhere under all that 'phantom tycoon' smoke?"

A wind gust skirts the glass, a shifting silver cloud casting geometric shadows on the charcoal wall behind Silas. He doesn't answer immediately. His eyes go to the city, scanning steel, light, the endless crawl of taxis and lives below. His reflection warps on the window—a man built for empires, himself haunted in the gleam.

"There are stories people tell to keep the world turning," he says at last, his voice low. "Sometimes those stories protect things the world isn't ready to see. They're easier than truth. They serve their purpose."

Every syllable is measured. Hana studies him, her lips tightening, a rush of past betrayals running through her blood—voices whispering you can't trust them, not after what happened last time. She's learned not to flinch in the face of power, but sometimes she wonders if the armor she grips so tightly keeps her from feeling anything at all.

"I said ruthless," she replies quietly. "But I can live with ruthless. What scares me is dishonesty—illusion dressed up as leadership. Power that's a curtain for something rotten underneath." Her fingers close around the mug, tension creeping from her hand to the rigid set of her shoulders. "I can handle the truth, Mr. Carver."

For a fragment, nothing moves. Silas's mask flickers, a split-second fracture opening at the edge of his mouth. The city glimmers behind him, the cold November sun catching on glass. He exhales as if remembering something he never lets touch the air.

"Sometimes power's just armor you wear," he murmurs, his eyes fixed somewhere far beneath the skyline, "because you have nothing left."

The words float out between them, hushed and heavy, tasting of black coffee and iron. An admission whispered for no one else, as if they might vanish if spoken above a murmur.

Hana's breath stirs the steam. Her skin tingles, the usual comfort she finds in banter fleeing under the weight of what lingers in Silas's voice. He looks unbreakable, yet there's a fracture running under the steel: something lost, something shored up by calculation and relentless routine.

Silence pools, thick and shimmering. The office becomes a quiet aquarium, the shimmer of city light blurring the edges of everything real and imagined. Hana feels raw—a stray nerve humming against the smooth leather chair, her thumb pressing unconsciously on the ridge of her scar. Inside, walls she's spent years crafting shift uneasily. She wants to demand more, to claw past the ghost stories and see the wounds beneath the headlines, but another part of her whispers caution. Last time she trusted this feeling, it split her open. Trust means exposure. Exposure means pain.

She wonders if Silas ever lets anyone see past the myth. If Victor Kane—the brilliant, predatory rival whispered about in the newsfeeds, and the wolves circling this glass tower—hunts him not because he is heartless, but because he dares to hold something precious and risk it every day. Is power for Silas a steely weapon, or just a battered shield to weather storms?

Hana lingers on his last words, tracing their shape in her mind. Sometimes power is just armor. She understands all too well—how identity can be performed, how you steel yourself before you step into a world eager to devour the weak. But what if, beneath all of it, she found something honest and defenseless?

A flicker of longing dances beneath her defiance. Not for the man the city worships or fears, but for the secret ache she sees blooming at the edges of Silas's composure. If she could reach past her own scars, if she could trust again, what might she discover in that shadowed space between their stories?

Their eyes catch, neither daring to blink or retreat. The city churns outside—a silent frenzy of horns and ambition and hope. Between them, trust vibrates, fragile and electric, every second teasing at the edge of some unspoken gamble. To stay is to risk; to withdraw is to lose the chance forever.

For the space of a heartbeat, an accord pulses—a shared understanding between two souls armored not just for battle, but for the loneliness after. The coffee sits untouched, cooling as the walls of the office seem less like barriers and more like glass sanctuaries poised to shatter or shelter, depending on what happens next.

Hana tips forward in her chair, the polished leather creaking beneath her. Manhattan sprawls behind Silas—a mosaic of ambition and secrets, glass slicing sunlight into brutal, almost fantastical angles. The air between them is laced with the rich aroma of spiced coffee and the faint, deliberate hush of a world where every word might be a weapon.

She breaks the hush, her voice low, threading a confession in the space between. "You know, in this city, anyone can find power if they're willing to trade enough of themselves for it. Trust, though? That's rarer than diamonds. And ten times more dangerous to lose."

The corners of Silas's lips almost move—just enough that suspicion warps to something like approval, or maybe it's just a fracture in his armor. He lets the silence turn dense as velvet before answering, his tone stripped bare. "Trust is a currency even I can't counterfeit. And I've tried." For a blink, his mask slips, the mythic phantom replaced by a man who's tasted the price of every secret he's ever bought.

At that moment, both reach unconsciously for their mugs. Hana's fingers hesitate above the porcelain, so close to his that a single move would bridge the charged gap—skin almost touching, neither retreating. The scent of cinnamon lingers. Her pulse thrums along her wrist, betraying nothing but this: One step closer, and the ground might fall away.

For a breathless second, city noise falls to a muffled, far-off throb. The empire beyond the glass seems to shudder, displaced by something intimate and electric. Then Silas—composed as ever—withdraws his hand, a motion too gentle to be called rejection and too careful to be an invitation. Hana's hand retracts with a fractional delay, the warmth trailing her to her core even as she steadies her breath.

She rises, her blouse catching the light, drawing her shields tight again. "Thank you, Mr. Carver," she says, threading iron into the syllables, her gaze bright with wild, new questions. "For the coffee. And the candor." Her tone dances that line between reverent and reckless, glancing back at the desk, the skyline, the charged air.

Silas stands, his silhouette severe against the morning sun slicing in gold through floor-to-ceiling windows. His eyes follow her—cool, unreadable, but hollowed now at the edges, as if he's counted every risk wrapped inside that nearness. In that liminal moment before goodbye, he seems less an emperor and more a man caught between horizon and precipice.

She crosses the floor—heels echoing like the closing notes of a sonata—fingers brushing the glass door. For a moment, Hana glances back. The city's roar creeps in, sharp and insistent, but inside the office, the quiet lingers, weighted and alive. Then the door shuts with a clean, precise click that feels suspiciously like the end of something innocent, or the opening of a threshold no one in this room will ever cross in reverse.

On the far side of the glass, Silas watches her shadow slip away, haunted, as if already mourning whatever unknown thing they've set in motion. He stands utterly still, surrounded by the artifacts of power—mahogany desk, digital maps, rare books—yet the only thing that seems real is the memory of her hand, impossibly close.

Hana stands in the corridor, the hush of executive privilege humming behind her, and inhales the foreign air of the empire. She wonders, just for a reckless heartbeat, what it would mean to fall toward a man like Silas Carver. If trust is as rare—and as ruinous—as she suspects, what then would she risk to take another step inside his world? There's a thrill trembling at the thought, a lure that tastes of danger and forbidden fire. Part of her craves the thrill, the twisted hope that someone could see the wounds she hides and not turn away.

Yet fear flickers right beside that longing. She's seen power steal souls, watched people snap under the weight of secrets and loyalty owed to the wrong gods. In Silas, she recognizes the edges of that same hunger, the same armor she's had to build for herself. Does she dare let it slip?

His rare, fractured smile replays in her mind, softer than rumor, more dangerous than threat. She remembers the near-touch, the static charge chasing down her spine, and her stomach flips in wariness and want. Letting anyone in—especially him—could unravel everything she's worked so hard to control. But the thought of never seeing behind his mask, never seeing if the phantom is just a man, terrifies her more.

They are two storms circling, each measuring the other for weakness. The city keeps roaring, the world goes about its business, unaware that inside a glass tower, the kindling for something catastrophic or beautiful has just sparked. Hana, steadying her breath, finds herself suspended on that edge—daring, in spite of everything, to hope.

Behind the door, Silas stands sentinel, hands braced on polished wood, his gaze fixed on the space she just left. The lines between power, vulnerability, and desire blur, each one more dangerous than the last.

Outside, the city belongs to men like him—men Victor Kane and Selena Voss would gladly destroy. But here, in this office, the most powerful thing in the world was almost, almost, just a touch.

Roses at Midnight

The elevator groans as it climbs, then judders to a stop on the fifth floor. A flicker of dying fluorescent bulbs paints the narrow corridor in sickly yellows and bruised blues, washing the decades-old wallpaper in a tired glow. Hana steadies her grip on the paper-wrapped takeout bag, keys clinking softly with each step past peeling doors and hollowed-out potted ferns. Her feet ache in her battered sneakers, soles half-numb from ten hours on her feet. All she wants is the hush of her apartment, perhaps soup she won't finish, the weight of the day melting away. There's curry leaking through the bottom of the bag, spicy warmth trailing her through the stale, humid, radiator-thick air.

Outside 5B, she stops short. Something interrupts the familiar—an arrangement, impossibly rich: black-and-red roses, petals luminous even in the gloom. Dew glitters on the tips as if dawn paused, trapped in midnight. The bouquet leans against the welcome mat her mother crocheted long ago—soft pastel yarn now dulled under city years. No note. Not the smallest slip of paper around the polished stems or the sleek black ribbon cinching the glassine shroud. Just roses. Just crimson and velvet shadows, fragrant as forbidden woods, staring up at her with deliberate intent.

A faint prickle rushes from Hana's scalp down her neck. The world narrows to roses, takeout, and twin rows of mailbox slots across the hall echoing with her heartbeat's thrum. She kneels, knees pressing against the faded sage carpet. One hand reaches, almost wary, brushing cold cellophane that shivers under her touch. The perfume—earth, wine, something like burning sugar—curls around her nose, thick and almost sweet enough to choke. She cradles the bouquet, tilting the cardholder atop. Nothing hides there. No signature, no lopsided "Get well soon," no marker-smudged "Sorry about earlier." Only absence, framed in thorns and silk.

A door opens further down—a neighbor's dog sniffs, claws on the tiles. Hana stiffens, clutching the flowers tight, knuckles whitening as if the roses might transform, bare their teeth, or vanish in a puff of illusion. The neighbor mumbles a greeting. She murmurs something noncommittal, half-turning from suspicion and habit. Shadows shift along the corridor, the soft drag of someone's coat, stale cigarette smell in the air. The world resumes its careless business, yet the bouquet tethers her to something just out of reach—an unknown, dangerous purpose.

She stands, bouquet pressed close. The brass numbers—5B—are lacquered with years of neglect, the '5' chipped at the corner. Hana traces them with her gaze, mind vaulting through memories of hands on hers, the smell of cologne mingling with newspaper ink, a gaze like stormlight behind glass. Only one person she knows would send black-and-red roses. The color of wreckage and rebirth. Of secrets—Silas's secrets.

There's an ache that pulses in her sternum. Exhaustion that's lived in her bones for weeks now tangled with bright, raw adrenaline. It's not just the risk of being sought by a man who walks in and out of power the way others cross streets. It's the fear that perhaps she hoped he would do something like this, even as she tries to convince herself otherwise. Roses mean devotion, perhaps, but black edges on petals whisper about danger, about things that bloom only after fire has claimed everything else. She thinks of rumors—Victor Kane's name sliding through café conversations and news crawls, whispers of anonymous threats against places Hana's never seen. Silas moved behind every one of those shadows, didn't he? Maybe just out of sight here, maybe closer than she dares guess.

Keys fumble against the lock. Her hands tremble, voice caught tight behind her teeth. She opens the door. City lights filter through threadbare curtains, dividing the cramped studio into pale gold and blue-black stripes. One long exhale fogs the air. Inside, the world's silence closes around her with a velvet weight. She pulls the door shut, bolts it once, presses the roses against her chest so hard the thorns just graze through the paper. The aroma is thicker here, intoxicating—like stepping into a memory she never made.

She stands in the hush, shoes scuffing the warped wood beneath, shoulder pressed to the door as if bracing against a coming storm. Her thumb runs along a petal soft as a bruise. Is this love? A game? A debt being collected? Protection, or a quiet promise that every step now leads deeper into a world watched by media hounds and men like Silas, men who make and break empires.

If someone asked—What do you fear most?—her answer would taste like these flowers: sweet at first, then bitter if swallowed.

She lets her head fall back against the door, squeezing the bouquet. Questions tick through her mind. If she called him, would he answer? Would he deny sending them? Or would his next gift not be flowers but something colder, harsher, meant to mark her as his or warn her away? Did Silas see her now, here, on the edge? Does he want her closer to his darkness, or is this an omen—a boundary she's not supposed to cross?

There, in the hush broken only by horns and distant sirens, Hana breathes in the roses. It's impossible to say which is heavier: hope or dread. She carries both with her into her patchwork sanctuary, the night made thinner by petals black as a secret and red as a wound. She does not speak, but the question pulses unspoken—what happens now, and what will she become under the shadow of the man who leaves no notes at midnight?

She closes her eyes, clutching the roses, and lets the city fade, knowing tonight nothing is truly safe.

Hana places the bouquet on her kitchen table, fingers tingling as the cold glassine crackles beneath her grip. The roses—so vivid and unnatural, their red so dark it's nearly black—stand in stark defiance to the battered wood and flickering bulb above. She opens her fridge with a soft sigh, contending with shelves crammed tight with half-eaten leftovers and dollar-store condiments, searching behind a bottle of cheap sriracha until her hand closes on the chipped ceramic vase. Even rinsing it, she notices the cracks, the thin gray lines spidering around her knuckles. Her hands tremble, just enough that warm tap water splashes onto the counter. She fills the vase, arranges the bouquet deliberately so the darkest blooms face her, then nudges it to the very heart of the table. Their perfume curls into the air, rich and unsettling—a scent so lush it feels like it might stain her tongue.

Her cardigan hangs loose off one shoulder, barely holding in what little warmth the apartment has left tonight. She sits, knees drawn up, chin nearly resting on the tabletop as she studies the roses. Outside, city silence presses in, muffled by brick and old glass. Every petal carries a pulse of memory: Silas in his shadow-thick office, the way his lips never quite softened even in a smile. The moment in the café, when his gaze swept her—slow, deliberate, as if he tasted secrets where others would only see exhaustion. The brush of his hand at the elevator, knuckles grazing her wrist and resting there too long.

No card. Just roses and darkness.

She runs her thumb along the torn edge of the bouquet's stem, murmuring to the quiet, "Why, Silas? Can't you say what you mean?"

Maybe he doesn't want to. Maybe he believes meaning is in the gesture, in the act of sending roses with petals black as a midnight bruise. Maybe he thinks she'll read the message and see only desire, or devotion, or a warning that the game is already underway. The vase shudders in her grip as she grapples with her own pulse, her breath hissing out between her teeth. Foolish to feel hunted and chosen at once.

Her feet scuff the floor. She presses her knuckles to her mouth, hunches lower, voice all but a sigh: "Is it a threat or a promise?"

And what does it say about her that she wants—so badly—to mistake one for the other?

She remembers what it was like—years back, before debts and betrayals, when love was something imagined in sunlight. The memory is sharp as vinegar, tightening her throat. She pushes it down and sits taller, keeping her eyes on those roses like they might open their petals, reveal their secrets, but of course they don't. Silas plays at truths wrapped in beauty and shadow; no wonder she can't decide if she wants to bolt the door or throw it open.

The television, left on for company, suddenly pops with a burst of static. Hana glances up, blinking as shadows from the screen flicker like ghosts across the kitchen wall. A news anchor's crisp voice slips under the door, talking about anonymous threats sent to powerbrokers and media empires—anonymous, the word rings, but she knows. The camera flashes a composite cityscape: skyscrapers cloaked in mist, a red dot pulsing over Midtown. The screen blares the Orion Brotherhood's name. Enemies circulate: Victor Kane, all steel eyes and old grudges; Selena Voss, cold as glass with her phoenix-branded arm; Damian Locke, a shadow that slithers through both boardrooms and alleys. Their ambitions choke the air and every glimmer of safety in it.

Hana stares down at the roses, the shadows of each bloom sprawled and elongated by the television's staccato light. The world feels suddenly smaller, ringed in by invisible strings—Silas's tangled web, or the Brotherhood's enemies tightening their hold on the city. In a place like this, a bouquet isn't only a gesture. It's a marker, proof that the line between gift and omen has already blurred—that even devotion here can become a weapon.

"Am I supposed to feel grateful?" she whispers. "Or just scared?"

The roses don't answer. Their perfume thickens, sweet as rot.

Her phone, silent in her bag, holds unread messages she can't bear to check, names she can't trust. She watches as the news segment cuts to footage of a masked courier slipping into a marble building—ominous, anonymous, inevitable. The broadcaster's voice lowers: destabilization, sabotage, criminal conspiracy. Hana's mind races, snared by the knowledge that her life is no longer her own. She thinks of Silas, orchestrating everything in silence, always one step ahead, and knows her fear is the same as her longing.

She leans forward, forehead settling on her folded arms beside the vase. A cheap candle wavers, casting the rim of light and spindly rose shadows across warped linoleum. The world outside keeps spinning, danger threading through every crack. Hana closes her eyes, breathing in the deep, unsettling sweetness, and waits—caught somewhere between the comfort of being seen and the dread of being marked.

The rooftop is a world apart: above the city's pulse, washed in the hush between midnight and storm. Silas stands at the edge, coat collar braced tight, the whip of wind threading through silver and black hair, sharp against his temples. The ruined neon sign at his elbow spits pale red at broken glass, painting his shoes in uncertain color. Below, Greenwich Village crouches in sleepy defiance. Across the street, Hana's kitchen window is a lone square of gold in a stack of gray and darkness.

Silas lifts binoculars, their smooth casing as cold as his hands. In the glass, her shape becomes clarity—a ghost outlined by the steady halo from a threadbare lamp. She moves with small, careful gestures, arranging the roses he sent: black and red, cut too perfectly, their petals as strange as secrets. She turns the bouquet in her slim hands, jaw set, brows knit. One moment she's frozen, the next she's pacing, lips moving in silent reckoning as if she could speak answers loose from the closed world around her.

He watches, heart clenched in the strange territory between pride and guilt. There is comfort in her presence, but only at a distance. His mind, always cataloging risks—enemies waiting beneath their own neon, Victor Kane brewing venom in media studios, Selena Voss cold behind government glass, Damian Locke prowling for leverage—spins out the permutations of what happens if she is seen to matter to him. That bouquet on her threshold is a flag in the dirt where shadows have always ruled.

A car horn blares far below, metallic and raw, but Hana does not startle. She sets the flowers in a chipped vase, water sloshing, candle flickering. He sees her mouth work around words, though the pane keeps her secrets. How would she curse him if she understood what shapes the gift carries? How would she break, or burn?

Silas lowers the binoculars, feels the press of bone and glass to his brow. He flexes his jaw, tension creasing the healed scar along his left cheek—pain, memory, warning. The wind stirs the hem of his coat, makes it thrash like a wounded thing. He shifts, one boot scuffing the tar. In this solitary theater, nothing conceals the weight of his choices.

There's a world where he steps off this rooftop and leaves Hana untouched: no roses, no secret meetings, no glances pinned across crowded rooms. She'd be safer, maybe even free to breathe in streets without eyes tracking hers. But in that world, he's only a ghost, an architect of emptiness—not the man who traced her sorrow, who hungers for her laughter in rooms where only power matters. He knows that longing has stripped other men bare, left them broken on the altar of threat, but still the wanting persists. Love, in his world, is both a fragile refuge and a dangerous fissure. It pulls, it unmoors, it exposes weaknesses Victor and Selena would salivate over.

He weighs the twin edges of devotion and obsession. Protection has a scent—cut grass, rose, steel. It's a presence hovering in the surveillance logs, the hacked feeds, the shadowed alleys where threats coil tight. But at what point does vigilance become a prison? Hana never asked for his shield. Would she rage if she knew her freedom comes shackled to the very man who vows to keep her safe?

He closes his eyes, picturing her fingers at the stem of each rose, oblivious to the thorns embedded deep beneath the lush display. The gesture is not innocent. Black roses for warning, red for desire—a secret code only partly meant to comfort. To love him is to stand in the path of storms that broke empires and remade men. He wonders when she'll taste the price in the back of her throat, when the beauty will congeal into fear.

Sometimes, when sleep eludes him, he imagines a peace where their worlds are simpler: two strangers with no debts to old blood or bitter allies, wandering the Village hand in hand, anonymous. But even in dreams, he cannot unmake himself. Everything he touches is claimed by shadows; her light can't banish the edges for long.

He should walk away.

Instead, he pulls deeper into the curtain of night, gaze fixed once more on the rectangle of warmth that contains her. This is the work of men like him—laying traps, leaving gifts, watching the cost mount up. He bites back old apologies. Hana can never know how many lines he's already crossed. If the Brotherhood's enemies—Victor Kane with his cold eyes, Selena Voss's political machinery, Damian Locke's threat in every grit-stained boardroom—ever lay hands on her, she'll need every ounce of his ruthlessness.

The moment tightens. He slips into shadow, coat drawn close, each footstep muffled by cold tar and old city dirt. One last glance toward the window—her silhouette caught in trembling candlelight—and then he moves, disappearing down the stairwell. The city below hums, oblivious, but Silas Carver is a wraith weaving through its arteries, swearing silent oaths into the wind.

Hana will never see him. Not tonight. Yet every minute, he's the watcher at her night, the danger and the devotion, the worlds she hasn't yet lost.

The First Kiss

The city pulses far below, blind to the storm crackling behind the penthouse's immaculate walls. Silas stands at the edge of his living room, the polished marble beneath his shoes cold as the tension thrumming in the air. A wall of glass frames the sprawl of New York—skyscrapers pricking the night, car lights seeping like tiny veins—but it's Hana standing across the room that holds his attention. Her presence cuts through the minimalist perfection with something raw and electric.

On the surface, every line of Silas's body conveys control: shoulders squared, hands relaxed at his sides, breath measured and slow. Inside, a different current pulses—tight, volatile, thrumming beneath skin and bone. He can see the steel in Hana's posture, the defiant set of her jaw, but he's seen the headlines: media hacks pouncing, whispers swirling from Victor Kane's camp, hidden thatches of danger circling closer. He doesn't want to cage her. He wants to shield her the only way he knows how—ruthlessly.

"Hana." His voice is quiet, as if reverberating just for her against the hush of high floors and city hum. "You're ignoring the risks surrounding this project. I know things you don't. You can't just brush aside my protection and walk blind through the fire."

Her eyes flash—light catching in their depths, reflecting metro moons and hard truths. She draws herself up, crossing her arms not in fear but in challenge. Her sneakers squeak softly as she squares up on the slick stone floor, the scent of spiced tea from some memory tonight barely masking the sharp tang of confrontation.

"So, that's what you call it?" Her words slice through the hush, clear and hot as a spark on gasoline. "Protection? It feels a hell of a lot like ownership. I'm not searching for a savior. I want you to let me decide where the lines are drawn." Every word is drawn taut with something just shy of fury.

He doesn't flinch. But something in him wants to. He feels the echo—an old wound, perhaps, part of himself shaped by secrets and the sting of past loss. Always too much at stake. Always someone ready to exploit weakness. And now, Victor's shadow pressing in; Selena Voss's name crisp on paper, cold in whisper. The world outside could turn on a word, and in this gleaming fortress, they are as exposed as ghosts on glass.

"You want autonomy. I want you alive, Hana. Is that so unforgivable?" The controlled chill in his voice cracks, just a fraction. "If you saw the threats—if you understood the names circling, you'd let me help. This isn't just about you or me. There are men out there—Victor Kane, for one—who would burn the whole city if it meant getting to the Brotherhood or anyone close to us."

She shakes her head, hair loose and wild, and the gesture is a flat refusal. "Don't put this on them. Whatever Victor Kane wants, or what Selena and the rest are scheming, I'm not property you can stash in a safe. Stop making my choices for me."

"Damn it, Hana, I'm trying to—" He catches himself, the words burning his tongue. He's not used to this: the feeling that anything could slip. That control could shatter. Silence falls, thick as velvet, broken only by the tick of a clock and the city's dull heart below.

Her voice softens just enough to bruise. "Is this who you are, Silas? Always watching from the shadows, always pulling strings? When do I get to breathe on my own terms?"

"Do you think I like this?" The confession spills—low, raw. "I don't sleep, Hana. Not while you walk these floors and my enemies sharpen their knives. Every instinct says move her, protect her, lock every door in this city. But I can't—" He draws a breath, heavy with decades of wariness. "I can't lose you to this world. Not when I... not when I could've stopped it."

Her shoulders tremble with rage—and maybe something else. "Maybe you can't stop everything. Let me take the risk. Or is this only about your curse, your precious control?"

He watches her lips tremble. She's fighting not just him, but the past they both drag behind them. He's never learned how to argue without wounding. For a beat, he almost reaches out—but she's already moving.

The suddenness with which Hana turns is like the snap of a snare, her breath jagged in the hush. The click of her boots—fast, furious across the marble—lands like gunshots in the cavernous room. Her spine is rigid, fists balled, every muscle tight with the urge to bolt. She leaves the curated warmth of the living area behind, steps fading into a hallway where city lights no longer reach.

Silas hesitates, jaw locked, the lines of his face carved by something harsher than anger. Frustration burns behind his eyes, but beneath it, terror claws. His need to protect tugs at every rule, every promise he's ever made to himself, the Brotherhood, the ghosts of parents lost to schemes and secrets. He cannot give ground. Not with men like Kane out there, not with Voss sniffing out any sign of weakness. The world is a chessboard, and Hana doesn't know all the rules.

He follows, measured and relentless, the echo of his shoes trailing her into the sepulchral hush of the corridor. Shadows paint his path—soft, predatory. The air shimmers with ozone and old regret.

Hana stops by the hallway's edge, reaching for her coat with a hand that trembles faintly, rage fighting for primacy over fear. His presence looms behind her—a force as much as a man, the tension strung so tight between them it feels as though the world might splinter. Her knuckles whiten on the coat's collar. He draws closer, silent, shadow swallowing shadow, distance measured now in heartbeats, not feet.

Hana's fingers brush the sleeve of her coat, her steps hungry for escape. The hallway's cool glow slices shadows across her skin; the penthouse is a sleek, silent witness to their fracture. Behind her, Silas moves—quiet as a storm before it breaks. His hand closes around her wrist, not harsh, but absolute. Under his touch, her pulse flares; his grip is iron wrapped in velvet.

She spins, fury sharpening every line of her face, but it's met by a gaze colder than steel, haunted by something unspoken. Their breaths tangle in the hush, audible against the silence of the city many floors below.

"Let go," she snaps, her voice frayed with danger and need.

"You walk out now, there's no guarantee you're safe." His words are flint, struck against stone. "You can't see every shadow waiting for you."

She yanks, but his hold is relentless, gentler than it should be, teasing out a warning.

"Silas, this isn't protection. It's a leash you won't let go of."

"I'd rather see you furious than see you vanish," he says, jaw tight, eyes scanning her face for something he cannot command. "You think I'm just trying to own you? You have no idea what's out there. Victor Kane's people, Selena Voss—do you want to be caught in their crossfire because of me?"

She glances down the corridor toward the gleaming door, chin lifted, defiance burning. "If you're so scared for me, trust that I know how to survive predators. I've done it before. I won't be one of your secrets, Silas—I won't disappear for you."

His grip tightens with a shiver of desperation, something trembling beneath his composure. For all his careful indifference, he cannot let her go. The composure is a lie.

He pulls her toward him. The soft light overhead flickers, painting them as brittle silhouettes cast against the polished wall. The city buzzes distantly through the insulated glass, the faint taste of ozone riding the air as if warning of a coming summer storm. He smells of vetiver and paper, the edge of cologne smothered beneath anxiety.

The moment before he kisses her stretches, breathless—a place where neither power nor surrender can rule.

Silas's lips find hers, urgent, bruising with need, shattering the distance he's spent a lifetime crafting. At first, Hana's body is stone, her fists pressed to his chest, unyielding. The press of silk against her knuckles, the hard thud of his heart beneath, makes her tremble. Her mind splinters—years of running, of building herself from salt and splinters—collide with the rawness of this moment.

But control gives way. Elbows weakening, fingers sliding upward, she curls her hands over his shoulders. Her body softens despite herself, drawn to the heat that unravels every wary thread inside her. The hallway's hush breaks with the scrape of her breath—part surrender, part plea.

He tastes her, and in her taste is the memory of nights spent hollow, of grief swallowed in the dark chambers of his life. Hana is the only real thing in a world spun from secrets and calculated shadows.

He's falling. He knows it—the recklessness, the shame, the greedy want that makes the Brotherhood's cold doctrines irrelevant. Every betrayal, every measured gesture built on expectation and fear, every sleepless night watching the skyline for threats—he buries it all behind the blur of her mouth against his.

And still, a warning howls inside him: you cannot have this and keep what you built. He imagines Victor Kane's eyes, calculating, the smile of Selena Voss as she sharpens knives in the dark. He imagines the cost.

Hana drowns and surfaces, longing and dread plaited in her chest. The heat of his kiss is an answer to her loneliness, but also a threat—because once, trust ruined everything she loved. What if he is only another mask, another man whose secrets write her into sorrow?

He breaks the kiss suddenly, breath stuttering between them. Her lips taste of rosehips and a little blood.

His eyes are molten, shadowed with secrets he's never confessed. "I am not the man you think I am." The words are stripped raw, spoken into the space where hope and fear collide.

For a heartbeat, they do not move. Hana's chest rises and falls, the sharp line of her jaw trembling as she blinks away the stars spinning behind her eyes. Silas's fingers loosen but do not release, their bodies stranded in the hush—a darkness brightened only by the city's distant, relentless lights.

The silence is absolute. The warning hangs in the air—a scar poised to break open.

Hana recoils, breaking from Silas's shadow as if she's just touched a live wire. Her hand still tingles—memory and sensation muddled, the echo of his grip burning where flesh met flesh. The marble at her feet chills her through her boots, and the air inside the penthouse now tastes metallic, sharp as blood on a bitten tongue. She stumbles back, pulse stuttering. Silas's words—"I am not the man you think I am"—slice deeper than the steel and glass surrounding them.

For a heartbeat, she stands at the threshold, fingers curled around the edge of the door. There's safety out there, maybe, or at least distance. Rain drums quietly against the balcony windows, each drop a percussion matching the riot in her chest. She could leave—she's done it before, running from locked apartments, hospital hallways, memories that pressed in like hands at her throat. But some part of her aches, wild and irrepressible, and under the pale city lights, she glances back. The silence between them stretches, heavy and brittle. Behind her, Silas is half-glimpsed—tall, unmoving, features all angles and shadow. Want and warning are written in the lines of his hands. His restraint is iron, the kind that could break or save her.

Hana's voice shakes with everything she can't say. "You can't just decide who I am. Not after that." Her chin lifts, a brittle spark under pressure.

Silas's reply is sanded soft, no less dangerous for its quiet. "You think I don't see you? I see all of it, Hana. That's why I—" He cuts off, regret and longing coiling in the air.

She turns from him before either can ruin the moment further. Each step along the bare hallway aches with the threat of goodbye. She drapes her coat over one arm, uncertain if she means to put it on or abandon it for good.

"I told you I won't be owned." Her words, barely above a whisper, drift in the hush.

He stays rooted in place, gaze locked on her.

The city calls—distant, glittering, wholly indifferent. She slips out to the balcony, leaving the threshold behind. Cold wind rushes up from the avenues far below, carrying the smoke and sugar tang of roasted chestnuts, the ozone bite of impending rain. The city's lights shiver in the puddles, murals splashed against wet glass and midnight.

Out here, her breath fogs in the rush of winter. Hana wraps her arms around herself, drawing her coat tight even though it does nothing for the storm inside. The memory of Silas's kiss—desperate, possessive, almost a plea—flickers on her lips. Her hand, marked by his touch, curls into a fist. Old arguments tangle with new wounds.

She stares down—not at the unfeeling city—wind needling her skin, heart thrumming a wild staccato. Her mind reels through the ways she's been broken: the ex who bled her dry for cash and trust, the betrayals that hollowed out faith until only bone remained, nights spent ducking shadows in cheap apartments, hands clinging to borrowed bedsheets like armor. Vulnerability had always been a risk too big to take. And yet, Silas's mouth on hers had asked her to try, just this once—had begged her not to run.

He lingers behind her, framed in the doorway, outlined by the faint golden spill of light. He doesn't close the distance. Not yet. His restraint is louder than shouting, an apology spoken in the tension of knuckles gone white. From this height, Hana can see everything and nothing: headlights streaming uptown, neon squiggles, the smudge of Central Park under bruised clouds. The world goes on. But in the glass separating her from Silas, their reflections are ghosts, almost touching.

She wishes she could hate him for the warning—not the man you think I am—but the ache in her chest is sharp with longing and terror. The walls she built for herself clang together, welded by fear. She's seen how love shatters. She knows what it's like to sleep with the enemy and wake up alone with regret as company. Her hand, pressed flat to cool metal, shakes with the urge to turn back—to let him in.

She sifts her memories for courage. If Victor Kane, with all the lies spun on the front pages, can set ruin in motion from across the city, and if Selena Voss can twist fate with a whisper, there's no safety in retreat. All roads lead to pain here. Yet Hana remains on the edge, caught in the undertow between the temptation of his arms and the memory that every embrace can be a trap.

A car horn blares, distant but insistent—a reminder that the world below thrives despite every secret war. She presses her lips together, breathes in smoke and hope. The chill doesn't abate. She closes her eyes for a second, sees not just Silas but every version of herself that's fought to survive—reckless, wounded, unbroken.

She opens them, then, and meets his gaze through the glass. No words pass. Just the sky between them, thick with longing and the threat of another fall.

Lines Crossed

The library looms, a steel-and-marble sanctuary carved atop the city's veins of neon and darkness. Every angle whispers of discipline: sharp lines, locked cabinets flush with the wall, a mahogany desk as broad as a shield. Floor-to-ceiling windows pour out the hushed spectacle of Manhattan—millions of glimmering lights, all distant and unreachable. The city's pulse only serves to enforce the library's hush. Inside, soft classical piano swells from hidden speakers—every note arranged, every shadow planned. The scent is faintly metallic, edged with the polished tang of old books and the subtle, living trace of rare orchids perched on glass shelves. There is nothing warm in this air, nothing to invite chaos or comfort.

Silas moves with a measured prowl, his tailored suit blending into the chiaroscuro. He gestures for Hana to move forward with the smallest flick of his hand. "We had unfinished business, Ms. Brooks." The words barely cut through the dim silence, intent slipping beneath the formality. He watches her reflection ghost across the glass behind her, city lights tracing the curve of her jaw.

Hana hesitates at the edge of the deep carpet, arms folded tightly across her chest. The mahogany shelves—packed with volumes too old to touch and dossiers bound in austere black—rise beside her. She angles her body away, shoulder first, trying not to seem defensive. But her eyes flicker to the locked cabinets and the faint red LED that glows atop a biometric safe. The music seeps in around her, a lull and a warning.

"Is this what you do with all your guests, Mr. Carver? Lead them somewhere no one can interrupt?" Her tone cuts, soft with an edge.

"Not all. Only when a guest proves herself... uniquely difficult to read." Silas's answer is silk over steel, his gaze steady. He stands close enough that the subtle silver at his temples catches the moody light. The line of his jaw is hard, but a tremor hides there—restraint crackling in the set of his mouth.

"I'm not difficult. I just don't trust boardrooms built on lies." Hana's laugh is soft—more breath than sound.

Silas's eyes darken. He closes the distance in three controlled steps, stopping a breath away. She stumbles a half-step back, the velvet drape brushing her spine, cool against her skin. Now, the city is behind her, relentless and unreachable, and his presence presses in from the front—an unspoken warning shadowed in the set of his shoulders.

He doesn't touch her. Not yet. He lets silence pool until even the music becomes background static—just the metronome to his pulse. For a moment, Silas is every inch the strategist: a man who knows every exit, every secret, and how to turn an encounter into a chess move. But tonight, the cold assurance is fractured. A dent forms in the armor.

He nods to the low table nearby, where a thin file sits atop a leather folio. "You want transparency. Fine. Ask me what's inside." As he reaches, his hand brushes hers—bare skin on skin, her knuckles cool and tense. The touch is inadvertent, but neither of them pulls away.

Hana's fingers splay reflexively, brushing against his. The accidental contact stills the room, tipping everything. Something cracks inside Silas—a restraint breaking, will snapping taut with the force of danger. He lets out a silent curse. Enough control. He cups her waist, fingers trembling only slightly, and pulls her closer.

His mouth claims hers—no warning, no lead-in. The kiss is raw, searching, desperate enough to unravel the soft, careful layers they both wear. Hana stiffens, then melts against him, one brief gasp swallowed by his lips. His hand at her waist holds her steady as the city spins unheeded behind them.

She tastes like cinnamon and coffee, like something alive and fighting. The world outside—the locked cabinets, the threat of rival moguls like Victor Kane, the orchestra of secrets behind every wall—falls away. For a moment, nothing penetrates the shield of glass and steel. His pulse throbs beneath his skin, sharp with the knowledge that he is giving something away.

Silas softens, just barely, teeth grazing her bottom lip. His other hand slides along her arm, every nerve exposed. The classical music muffles beneath their breath, a mere suggestion now—routine and order slipping into the current of this storm.

They break apart slowly. The air between them pulses, thick and heavy, each of them catching their breath like swimmers pulled from deep water. Neither speaks. Shadows cut their faces—his, carved with conflict; hers, flushed, lips parted.

Hana keeps her eyes pinned to his, searching for the man beneath the damask control. He stays close, one hand still hovering at her waist. Both know this is a line crossed—one that cannot be easily unwound, no matter what bargains are struck, no matter how many secrets the night keeps.

Beyond the glass, Manhattan keeps glittering—indifferent to power, to longing, to ruin. Inside, the library reflects Silas's world: perfectly controlled, but thrumming now with a danger its master can hardly name. In the hush, the silk of the drapes and the chill of the marble serve as reminders—this room is a fortress, but for whom?

The silence stretches, trembling with what might happen next, their bodies illuminated by the fractured patterns of city light and the flicker of something elemental neither of them dares name.

Hana staggers back, her hand clumsy against the cold edge of Silas's oak table, breath shuddering in her lungs. She presses shaking fingertips to her mouth, as if to trap the heat of that fevered kiss before it can scald her resolve. Around her, the penthouse library holds its breath—books climbing the walls, the air tainted with wood polish and the faint, uneasy trace of Silas's aftershave. The city glows beyond the windows: a thousand lit windows, every one a silence, every one a secret.

She tries to steady herself, to appear less undone. Her back is sticky with nerves, skin prickling beneath her thin blouse. Classical piano murmurs from hidden speakers above, each note a phantom reminder of the man spooling tension behind her, drawing her closer with gravity she can't fight.

Inside, Hana's mind splits, the present battered by the ghosts of her past. A rush of ugly memories hits—her ex's voice, abrasive in the freezing shadow of their old apartment. "You're lucky anyone wants you. Grateful, remember?" The memory curls inside her chest like spoiled milk. Then—older, icier—men with wolfish smiles at her first job, eyes full of invitation and threat, reminding her how easy it is to be prey in a beautiful dress. Those men didn't hold secrets the way Silas does, but their power was no less suffocating.

She breathes in, tasting anxiety on her tongue, bitter as burned espresso. That other memory rises: the sickening thud of the debt collector's fist on her door, a gut-deep fear that never leaves. Even now, the weight of their threats lingers in her bones, an invisible bruise. Scar tissue above her left brow tightens, as if recalling the night she'd tripped on broken glass while running from another argument, another demand for money she didn't have. Every scar's a warning label, each mistake a lesson—don't trust the powerful, don't hope for rescue, never need anyone who holds a weapon in the shape of a pr omise.

She glances at Silas. Powerful men walk like they own the air, but just now, his fingers tremble at his side, knuckles white as they curl around the file he never quite grabs. The mask he wears fractures for a second: control faltering, vulnerability threading through his usually impenetrable eyes. In that flicker, Hana sees not the strategist—but the man. That makes him more dangerous, not less. Because the hungry and the hurt are always hoping for a soft place to land, even when they know better.

"Why—why did you do that?" Her voice is thin, splintered, not trusting itself.

Silas's answer is a hush against the tension. "You think I know?" His words hang heavy, like the dust motes swirling through weak lamplight. "You're... I can't seem to stop."

She shakes her head, tucking her arms around her ribs, as if holding herself in place. The hem of her sleeve brushes the scar—flesh knitting over old pain, reminders stitched in silence.

"Don't say things like that. Don't—" Hana hesitates, choking back the urge to run. "Don't act like I'm... something you can't control. I've seen where that road goes."

Silas's reply is almost a whisper. "I'm not like him." Silence stretches, the city heartbeat pulsing faintly through the glass.

Hana closes her eyes, letting the echo of that kiss crash through her. The part of her that craves warmth wants to cling, to settle into the promise of his arms and forget the world. The part that remembers sleepless nights, emptied accounts, teeth gritted through humiliation—she wants to run. Survival has always been movement: don't stop, don't get caught, don't believe. Never want too much.

But the ache in her chest isn't just fear now. Silas, with his ruined tenderness and terrible precision, has stripped some layer from her she thought would never crack. There is need here—horrifying, exquisite—as dangerous as any debt. She's not sure if it's hope or a waking nightmare.

Every warning she rehearsed since she first glimpsed the cut of his jaw, every late-night vow to keep her heart locked away—they all seem inadequate. This isn't some careful withdrawal. This is a burning: a leap into something consuming.

She stands there, listening to her own uneven breaths. The space between them vibrates with things left unsaid. Hana's skin tingles where his lips pressed, memory branded into flesh. Logic wars with longing: you can't survive surrender, you can't bear another disappointment. But—how can she bear never knowing if something softer waits beneath his steel defense?

The classical music falters on a minor chord. Hana opens her eyes, and the library lights cast long shadows across the polished floor, trapping her between history and possibility. Silas waits, uncertain, the city's midnight haze painting his profile in bruised silver. In the hush, every past bruise and hard lesson converges with the unbearable truth of this moment: even as fear claws at her, she can't walk away. Not yet.

Her gaze latches onto his, silent, questioning. In this charged pause, with the world beyond the glass indifferent to their war, Hana's destiny hangs trembling between fight and flight.

Silas Carver stands with one hand braced against the carved edge of the library desk, the other loosely curled at his side as if holding on to composure by slender threads. Moonlight licks through the glass, painting the sprawl of Manhattan in metallic bruises; the city below pulses, heedless of the collision trembling behind these soundproofed panes. The air in the penthouse vibrates with silence, thrumming against the soft sob of a cello piping through hidden speakers—a requiem haunting marble and velvet drapes.

Hana sits suspended on the thin ledge between candor and retreat. The scent of him—clean cedar, faint warmth of bourbon, something sharper lurking underneath—curls through the night. His suit jacket hangs just so, wrinkled along one shoulder, a faint silver glint threading through his hair. What startles her isn't the evidence of strain but the hint of weariness that pulls the lines at his mouth downward. For once, Silas Carver's armor doesn't fit quite right.

His shoulders drop a fraction, breath rattling into the hush as he gathers himself from the inside out. "You'd think," he mutters, voice knotted with a rasp that startles them both, "all these years learning how to outmaneuver kings and predators would've taught me how to keep my distance—how to keep everything in its proper place."

She doesn't answer, doesn't need to. The precise way she steadies herself, forearms gripping the far edge of the table, betrays how close the ground feels to giving out beneath them. Her eyes search his face for a sign—weakness, cruelty, the method behind his hunger. He looks back, gaze stripped of its usual ice. Only exhaustion and a glint of something more fragile—yearning, perhaps, or the recognition of his own undoing.

A shiver slips between their chests, a warning pitched in the minor key of old grief and new want.

Silas seems to sense it too. The hand at his side lifts, fingers flexing once before he lets it fall over a closed dossier—Victor Kane's name scrawled in a bold, impatient hand flashing briefly before he covers it with his palm. The city's most dangerous rival waits in those sealed files, but all Silas feels now is the living risk at arm's length.

"I was prepared for a thousand things," he whispers, eyes fixing on Hana so fiercely that the room recedes. "The attacks from politicians, the threats Kane and Selena Voss throw at the walls...every campaign, every accusation. But I never counted on you, Hana. I never counted on this."

There's a tremor in his voice, a catch he cannot swallow. For the first time, strategy fails him—the blueprints for survival torn to ribbons by a woman with scarred eyebrows and the scent of burnt coffee trailing her skin. His fingers drum once on the desk's surface. Hana's hand twitches. She's as desperate to bolt as she is to touch him. The library lights flicker, condensing shadows around their feet.

"You make it sound like some affliction," she says, voice silked over iron, half-confession, half-dare. "You've built a world out of locked doors and war rooms. Maybe you just never expected any of them to open from the inside."

Silas turns his head, jaw tightening. Something inside him ripples, brittle and raw. The mask has slipped entirely now, laying bare the toll—the sleepless nights surveilling enemies, the weight of coded secrets cinched around his ribs like chains. The world expects omnipotence. But right now, Hana sees only a man bracing against the tide.

"Don't," he says, a plea hidden in roughness, "don't think you're safe here. Not from me. Not from what I am. Every time I try to keep that line in place—" He falters, searching for the tactician's lexicon and finding only the aching diction of longing. "You walk right over it. And I let you. I can't help myself, Hana."

"Maybe you can't," she murmurs. "But neither can I. So what do we do now—just drift until one of us drowns in all this?"

A fraught silence crushes the distance between them. Hana's thumb skims over the faint scar on her brow, gaze unblinking, unafraid. Silas inhales sharply, a soft hiss caught between threat and surrender.

"It's dangerous," Silas forces out, low and unvarnished, "not just because of the things I keep locked—because of Kane and Selena and a hundred others who would burn us for the power they taste in blood—but because you make me want..." He doesn't finish. The wanting is everywhere—in their haunted faces, in the air trembling around them, in the fact that neither turns away.

Her voice slips between the library's shelves, quiet as a spell. "Then say it. Say what you want and let whatever comes after be your answer."

They hold each other's gaze. The city's midnight haze swallows the towers; the world narrows to shallow breaths and a glass wall smeared with ghostly reflections. Vulnerability, jagged and new, unspools across Silas's expression. In Hana's eyes, he sees the same need—the same terror, coiled together and waiting for permission.

Nothing will be the same now. Not after this. Not with the storm gathering outside, nor with the knowledge that their barricades are already falling, one longing glance at a time.

Hana backs away, the plush carpet silent beneath her shoes, breath catching when her spine nearly grazes the chilled glass doors. A threadbare dawn presses its pale light against the skyline, drawing the city's towers in haunted blue and silver. Out there, life is igniting by the minute: delivery trucks humming, streetlights lost to sunrise, a city that never considers what's unfolding in this high-lit cage of marble and velvet. Yet here, time stalls. The scent of old paper and the faint tang of Silas's cologne drift through the hush.

She lingers, one palm splayed on the brass handle, knuckles white, refusing to look over her shoulder just yet. Behind her, she can feel Silas watching, every heartbeat stretching and pulling at the thin seam that keeps her from unraveling.

Silas's voice lands in the air, softer than she expects, rough with something unspoken. "Some lines don't disappear, Hana. Not once you cross them. There are things you can't unsee—or peel away again."

She doesn't answer right away. The hum of his words seems to shudder through her bones, as if some hidden alarm—one she's always ignored—has finally started blaring beneath her skin. Her gaze passes over the cityscape, rooftops bathed in the first spill of gold, so far removed from the ruthless violence his world conceals. Out there, the world belongs to the innocent and the oblivious. Here between his words, it's only wolves and careful prey.

She glances back, just enough to catch the storm behind his eyes—eyes not made for daylight, too silver, too knowing. His expression flickers: something desperate, something protective, tangled up with warning. The script they've lived by, all those cautious negotiations and measured pauses, feels burned away in the new morning.

For one suspended moment, neither of them speaks. The only noise is the symphony's faint final movement—a minor-key cello, a sustained note, unresolved as everything between them.

Her jaw stiffens, but she meets his gaze anyway. "You don't get to decide what I can handle," she manages finally, her voice more fragile than she likes. "Or what happens next."

He exhales. The sound is almost a laugh, nearly a sigh, breaking the standoff. "That's the problem," he murmurs. "You can handle more than you should have to." For the first time, doubt saturates his tone.

She doesn't let herself be softened by it. "You want me on the other side of that line, and you're terrified of what it means. For you. For me."

Silas's hands flex as if he's fighting the urge to pull her close again, to impart significance with touch instead of words. For once, he doesn't. "I'm not the man you think I am," he says, nearly a whisper, more confession than excuse.

Hana's head bows. The creases in the glass door shimmer with trembling light. Every instinct tells her to run before regret becomes inevitable, before scars turn to shackles. But the pull, the ache to stay—just a heartbeat longer in this dangerous clarity—is almost unbearable.

Silas doesn't move. Shadows curl around his feet as dawn lifts the color out of the city, leaving them suspended between darkness and day. The world is changing outside and between them both—fragile, merciless, ripe for consequence.

She wants to bolt, to save herself, but stands pinned in a liminal space, craving answers she knows he won't give. What might be waiting if she steps through that door—ruin or something braver? She can't help but wonder if trust, real trust, is built from such moments:

not from certainty, but in the space after disaster, where both people are stripped bare.

She pictures the future as a corridor made of glass and mist: on one side, solace, the relief of being alone again; on the other, the jagged thrill and the peril of belonging to someone who terrifies her by seeing her, truly seeing her. She sifts through memories: debt collectors' harsh voices, her ex's cruel accusations, nights spent guarding her secrets like currency. All of it pressing her to retreat—to stay safe, stay invisible. But she's so very tired of safe.

The city yawns beneath her, half-dreaming still. Above, the sun claws silver from the horizon, promising nothing. A thousand possible lives spool from her fingertips. Every one costs something.

She glances once more at Silas, cataloguing the lines of exhaustion etched into his features, the silent plea in the tension of his stance, the thundercloud secret behind his solemn eyes. A fragile promise hums between them—unspoken but heavy. Maybe if she steps away, it will shatter. Maybe if she stays, it will ignite.

Her fingers curl around the brass handle. Her hand shakes. One slow breath, then she turns the latch. The door glides open without protest, flooding the threshold with brittle dawn.

She pauses, her silhouette carved by light and empty space, longing and dread coiling in her chest. For a flickering second, she hovers—then, finally, slips into the awakening corridor. The door swings to a hush behind her, sealing the room, and Silas, into solitude.

He stands unmoving as the new sun seeps over the penthouse. Golden light slants across the bookshelves, painting harsh stripes on the marble floor, while outside, the world stirs, oblivious. Somewhere below, antagonists—Victor Kane, Selena Voss, Damian Locke—move the pieces, their hidden war scraping closer. Between the walls, all that's left is the echo of a kiss and the dawn's raw promise, staking its claim on two souls who may have just begun their undoing.

Dinner with the Brotherhood

Hana lingers outside the great oak doors, her palms damp, half-wishing for thunder to roll and draw the mansion into darkness, granting her a moment longer in anonymity. But she pushes forward—two steps, three—her heels silent on marble that gleams almost blue under the cut of candlelight. Inside, the dining room opens like a secret garden for the powerful: velvet-backed chairs pressed into snowy white tablecloths, gilded candelabras flickering, and portraits of unsmiling men and women—generations of power—peer down from towering walls. Beyond, glass windows consume the city's dusk: a spray of diamond lights, towers pricking the sky, all of Manhattan sprawled beneath the Orion Club.

Centuries of ritual and money sweep through this room; it's in the chill of the polished stone, the heavy silver, and the way every wine glass stands at soldier's attention. The Brothers' table runs long, wide as a river, its dark wood unbroken but for burnished patterns like knots in an ancient map. Everything here is arranged—seating, silence, laughter—with the precision of a strategist in battle. Belonging isn't offered; it's earned in brushstrokes and measured words, under the gaze of history itself.

At the head of the table, four men turn as if summoned by her breath. Caius, nearest, arches a brow—a silent greeting sharpened by centuries of breeding. His suit fits like armor, formality clinging to his posture. Lucien's half-smile cuts warm, a flash of camaraderie that doesn't linger long. Darius, all quiet calm and dark eyes, nods as if in court, measured and kind. Orion—every edge of him a counterpoint to the others—tips back his chair, one long arm tossed carelessly along its spine.

"Hana, you made it. Right here—Silas saved you the best seat," Orion calls, his voice bright as city light on water. A hint of mischief, of challenge—the words ripple down the table.

Hana freezes, tightness coiling in her chest, every muscle recalling a lifetime as an outsider. The doors shut with a sigh behind her. For a moment, she is the interruption—the stray note in a symphony nobody dares question. She squeezes her purse, her fingers whitening.

Seraphine rises first. She wears a smile that feels like summer's promise, chestnut curls tumbling as she closes the distance. "You get used to the drama—it's mostly smoke and mirrors," she says low enough for only Hana to hear.

"Hana, come," Amara urges from behind, her hand gentle on Hana's elbow. Elara flanks the other side, her touch light but sure, her eyes soft with solidarity.

They guide her forward—the unspoken welcome in shared glances—and introduce themselves with the ease of women who have built their own realm inside tradition's strict lines.

"Seraphine. And this is Amara; Elara's on your right. If you sit next to Silas, we promise no one will bite—at least, not tonight," Seraphine teases, her voice coaxing a hesitant smile from Hana.

"Only if you keep the wine flowing," Amara adds, wry, with a glance at Caius that draws the faintest smirk from the ice-eyed financier.

She takes her seat beside Silas's empty chair, her heart thundering so loudly she almost misses the orchestra of voices, the soft clink of cutlery, the subtle rustle of fabric against velvet.

"Caius, did you re-sort the entire wine list again?" Lucien leans across the table, his eyebrows raised. His tone drips with affection—and a little disbelief.

"You prefer chaos, Lucien. Some of us have standards," Caius replies, dry as winter air.

Darius, low-voiced, adds, "The real question is whether Orion's latest app will crash before dessert or after."

Orion grins. "Hey, you want dinner—or you want to live in the future? Progress is messy, doc." He flicks a napkin at Darius, who catches it without flinching.

"I'll take messy over boredom," Darius shoots back. "But the kitchen staff are betting on a system reboot by midnight."

Lucien laughs. "At least it's not your heart he's tinkering with tonight, Darius."

Orion flashes a wink at Hana. "We try to keep things interesting. Most nights, anyway."

Light rings through the room, laughter cresting and falling until warmth pools like sunlight under the chandelier. At the far right, Silas sits—silent, composed, his face carved from shadow and resolve. He folds his napkin with slow care, every movement precise, a man drafting invisible blueprints while the world spins beside him.

Hana sneaks a glance at him; he offers a smile—small, unreadable, and gone before she can return it. The air between them shivers, anticipation caught somewhere between warning and welcome.

She settles into her chair, her pulse still fluttering, as glasses are raised and more laughter curls across the polished table. She wonders, not for the first time, what it means to belong at a table like this: inside the club where treachery and loyalty mix in the wine, where the echoes of Victor Kane's threats and the shadows of Selena Voss and Damian Locke linger beyond velvet drapes.

All around her, the rituals of power unfold—every smile, every sidelong look, every elegant touch of fork to plate a sign of the old, unbroken order. Each gesture a marker, each place at the table hard-won, drawn from centuries' worth of decisions and quiet wars fought behind closed doors.

Hana's breath slows. The fear remains, right there under her ribs, but woven with it is something new—a whisper that she could make this place hers, even if only for one trembling heartbeat. The world outside has always been sharp; here, in this glittering den, she feels the danger differently: as invitation, as test.

The laughter rises again, and Hana lets the sound fold over her, steadying herself as she glimpses the possibility—a seat at the table, if she dares to take it.

Candlelight gathers in little pools on the snowy tablecloth, tongues of flame flickering in tall glass hurricanes set precisely between crystal and silver. The Brotherhood's grand dining chamber absorbs dusk through towering windows, the city beyond now only a shivering echo—cool blues and golds mirrored off polished marble tile. The scent of early summer roses, sharp with memory and opulence, lingers beneath notes of grilled vegetables and warm bread as the salads arrive in shallow porcelain bowls.

Seraphine leans into Hana's side, curls slipping forward, her voice a silvery hush conspiratorial enough to chase away formality. "My first dinner here? I tipped an entire glass of Chardonnay into Caius's lap. Thought maybe if I talked finance, they'd forget, but I just started quoting New Yorker cartoons. I still die a little remembering it."

Hana, fork poised mid-air, blinks away the tension coiled tight behind her eyes. The velvet-backed chair supports her, but she feels every muscle tight as piano wire. The table stretches on forever, draped in white linen and guarded by the portraits of men—stern, shadowed, armored in the trappings of power. On her left, Amara's laughter is a peppery warmth. "Caius still checks his seat twice before he sits—old wounds," Amara teases, her eyes gleaming. "But that's nothing. You want secrets?" She drops her voice as Orion mock-glares from across the table. "Ask about Orion's commitment to corporate meme warfare."

Orion winks, leaning over his untouched greens. "I stand by my gifs. When the board can recite SpongeBob references, we all win."

Seraphine's smile curves sly at the corners. "Darius once tried to meditate through a shareholders' revolt. Didn't even blink. Calm on the outside—inside he was probably reciting his own obituary."

Darius huffs a laugh, his accent softened by the candlelight. "Just didn't want to spill any more wine than Seraphine managed."

Elara, soft-voiced and sure, edges her chair closer to Hana's right. She tucks a strand of hair behind her ear, a gesture of invitation. "The truth is, no one is born knowing how to live here. Seraphine and Amara held me up, literally, when the press came for me—before I'd even had dessert. Sometimes you fall. Sometimes you laugh about it, eventually."

Amara's hand drapes over Hana's, light as a promise. There's comfort in the press of her palm and the glint of crescent-moon ink at her wrist. "We're used to taking turns being lost, Hana. Even on the glittering nights."

Across the table, Silas sits—immaculate, composed, a study in shadow and restraint. He doesn't speak to the women's chatter. His attention is measured, his head slightly bowed as he studies the rim of his wineglass, his knuckles whitening as he turns it. But every few breaths, his gaze finds Hana's face, still and searching, as if he's trying to solve an equation only he can see. There's thunder, bottled and waiting, somewhere behind those eyes.

Seraphine leans back, her voice turning gentle and teasing all at once. "Ignore them. We all fell on our faces, one way or another. At least you came in standing tall. The hard part is just letting yourself laugh about it."

"Easy for you, now," Hana mutters, but the edge in her voice softens in Amara's presence. The laughter from the table's other end rises in a wave. For a moment, Hana is outside herself, watching—her hand steadying the fork, the skin on her knuckles faintly shiny beneath the lights, the pressure of three unfamiliar women rooting her to earth and now, this table. The warmth is a rare, stinging thing.

Dialogue fades in and out like the tide: the men are debating city politics now, sharp-edged and quick; the women's talk returns to old scandals and holidays gone awry, to who was worst at cards and who cheats at charades. There's a rhythm to it—trust handed in small, edible pieces, honesty offered in the safe shadows between dangers.

Elara's whisper slips through, silk against glass. "You know, for years I thought I had to be perfect, or they'd figure out I didn't belong.

Turns out, nobody in this room does. You can breathe, Hana. You belong as much as any of us."

A silence falls between courses, broken only by the brush of stemware against lips, the fire's soft hiss, and distant city horns. Hana's shoulders finally, timidly, unspool. Her lips part with surprise as a genuine laugh escapes, lighter than she expects—unbidden as sunrise.

She glances up. Silas is watching, utterly still, the mask of his serenity brittle as pressed ash. His eyes don't smile. There is something fierce there, some warning—trust is not a thing easily traded in these rooms built on secrets. Hana's heart thrums, wound tight again, torn between these women's circle of hands and Silas's solitary gravity. Across the kingdom of linen and roses, between shadow and safety, she finds herself dancing at the edge of hope and wariness, each breath both invitation and defense.

The sweet aroma of espresso and burnt sugar drifts through the grand dining chamber as dessert arrives, shadows dancing in ripples over the marble. Outside, the city becomes a crown of glass and neon, smudged gold and blue behind the balcony's closed doors. Candlelight carves fragile halos around the Brotherhood, steady hands and expensive watches reflected in gleaming stems of crystal.

Caius's eyes narrow, his lips curving with wry amusement as he stabs a fork at his plate. "Tell me, Lucien, are you still counting your blessings after that little coup last year? Or are you revising your will again?"

Lucien leans back, his composure as sharp as the black suit he wears, steepling his fingers in mock solemnity. "I keep an attorney on retainer for every Brotherhood emergency. I even double-booked one last night after your text." He nods toward Darius, a sideways grin on his face. "At least I've kept out of the hospital scandals. Mostly."

A low rumble of laughter breaks the brittle hush. Darius lifts his chin, a muscle ticking in his jaw. "Don't drag me into your mess, Blackwell. I've got nurses threatening walkouts, half a hospital in lockdown, and the privilege of explaining it all to Board members who'd rather set the place on fire than admit to a mistake."

Orion, sprawled at the far end with the effortless arrogance of the night's youngest king, twirls his spoon. "Hey, at least you're not me. Didn't you see the headline this morning? Apparently, I'm still spamming tech journalists with pictures of my dog in sunglasses. You'd think a cyber hack was the end of the damn world."

The banter ripples outward, brushing laughter past trembling candles, and for a moment, the tension softens. But Hana feels it gathering back—like static in the velvet air. Her hand rests near her water glass, her fingertips drumming a tattoo against porcelain she hopes no one hears. She watches the men trade glances, each one landing a touch too sharp, a second too long.

Across the table, the women lean into their own quiet conversation. Seraphine's eyes flick up, searching the brothers' faces, while Amara smooths crumbs into a napkin with unnecessary precision. Elara offers a gentle squeeze to Hana's arm, her smile brittle at the edges. Under the laughter, there's something bruised.

Hana listens to the subtle snatches of breath between jokes, the almost imperceptible tightening of a jaw, the guarded sweep of a glance. She catches it all. These men wear their scars deftly cloaked in humor, but if you look—really look—you see what's left after the scandals and betrayals, every headline a taxed nerve.

A world like this: all ritual, power, velvet privilege, and glass—yet nothing is soft. Even laughter feels rehearsed, tight at the seams. Hana finds herself cataloging the lines around Silas's eyes, the set of Lucien's shoulders, the paleness of Darius's knuckles as he clutches a fork.

She wonders, not for the first time, how long this sanctuary can hold. How much weight brotherhood bears before the marble fractures and the world pries its secrets out with knives and wiretaps. Victor Kane's name, whispered months ago in Silas's study—fierce rival, media saboteur—ripples through the back of Hana's mind. Selena Voss, the senator with ice-blue eyes and a taste for control, and Damian Locke, always circling in the outer dark, striking where the cracks are deepest. Hana doesn't know all their faces yet, but she knows dread's outlines in the men's silence.

Silas sits at her right, a figure etched in shadow and dimmed crystal. All through the exchange, he does not join the jibes. His thumb traces the shape of a rose, invisible, on the linen beside his wine glass. His jaw is set, every muscle telegraphing the restraint it takes not to let his thoughts seep through.

Lucien angles a smirk at Orion. "Remind me not to update my firewall if you built it."

Orion fires back, "Hey, mine only leaks private memes, not federal indictments—unlike Caius's old firm."

Caius arches a brow. "I see my reputation precedes me. Darius, next time, you're responsible for the icebreakers."

Darius's mouth twists into an echo of a smile. "I'll bring defibrillators."

The laughter limps along for a beat before silence slides in, filling the space between candle flames and silver. Silas's gaze lifts—cold, slate gray under the flicker. Something in him seems to shutter, drawing tight and far. Hana senses it, the way frost creeps over glass. Her chest aches, instinctively reaching for the warmth that seems to be bleeding out of the room.

There is a terrible beauty in the way these men gather—a constellation scorched and trembling. Hana feels it all pressing in: the legacy they defend, the secrets that could devour them. What would it mean, she wonders, to belong here, to tie her fate to these shadows? There is safety in their unity, but it's fragile, a chain always straining for one s lip.

As the final silver tray is cleared and the mansion's windows burn against the night, Silas rises. He does not speak, but the arch of his body, the way his brothers match the gesture, signals the end. Around the table, subtle nods—a private oath exchanged not in words but in glances, tension soldered beneath polished exteriors.

While the others drift away, Hana lingers, drawn to Silas's silhouette as he moves toward the balcony, his shadow swallowing the last of the light. There's an unspoken promise in the air—storms are coming, and the first crack in the sanctuary may already be running straight through her heart.

Hana's Past Returns

The late afternoon light drips through the café windows, caramel and gold, dusting Hana's skin as she wipes a ring from a sticky table beside the glass. The room buzzes—machines whirring, the aroma of burnt espresso grounded by a hint of cinnamon and bread—but her focus is splintered, her thumb nervously vibrating against the battered corner of her phone.

The cracked plastic back of her phone is warm, slick with sweat. A new message burns up from the broken screen:

You owe me. Today. Or everyone finds out. You know what I mean. Don't make me come in there, Hana.

Her chest contracts. For a moment, the world narrows to the old, familiar rhythm of dread. Her blood beats behind her eyes. She tastes metal—a taste she knows from every nightmare and morning after. She reads the words again and again until they etch themselves behind her eyelids, his threat a coil pressed tight against her ribs.

Three years, she thinks, letting her fingers tremble only for a second. Three years since she'd sworn never to hand over her power, never to play the frightened girl with nowhere to run. Debt, secrets, mistakes—her shadowed companions. But now the past is hunting her in daylight.

The bell above the café door jangles, laughter tumbling in with a wave of regulars. Hana's hands move on autopilot—clean, polish, smile. She glances up. Across the street, framed by brick shadows and city grime, her ex waits. Still tall. Still all predatory nonchalance. He's dressed too well for this neighborhood, pale eyes fixed on her through the window, a slow smirk blooming on his mouth. The street teems with people between them, but when his gaze meets hers, the crowd blurs and falls away.

He leans, the gesture casual. He drags a thumb over his throat—slow, deliberate. For a second, her knees threaten to buckle. Only she knows the meaning: don't cross me again. Her pulse hammers, panic tightening her grip on the phone until the plastic creaks. She feels the weight of every moment he held her choices hostage, every time she believed escape was a fantasy.

She blinks hard and sets the rag aside, sliding her cracked phone into her apron. Through the kitchen's swinging door, the air is thick with coffee grounds and roasting sugar. She breathes in—deep, steady—until she can taste her own resolve blooming bitter as burnt caramel. Telling herself, Not this time. She won't let him see her falter.

She pushes open the back door into the alley. The city's heartbeat is louder here, trash bins stacked against frost-scarred brick, the tang of stale beer and cigarettes. Hana circles, shoes scrabbling on loose gravel, catching the edge of the wall as she rounds the corner. Her ex is there, leaning in the shadow, arms crossed, the message clear in the curl of his lip.

"What do you want?" Her voice is flat, but the sting creeps in around the hard edges. "I'm not giving you anything."

"You always say that." He steps forward, blocking the mouth of the alley. "But we both know you're too soft to let things blow up. You want me gone, Hana? Pay up. Or I talk."

"Try," she spits, the word ricocheting off brick and echoing down her backbone. "You don't scare me anymore. I'm not your problem to solve. Find someone else to bleed dry."

He laughs, a low hum barely louder than the distant siren rounding MacDougal Street. "You play tough. Cute. I'll give you tonight."

His gaze lingers on her face, cataloging fear, hunger, hope—then drifts over her shoulder, dismissing her like a game he's already won. She senses the pull of old habits, the urge to shrink, yield, beg for mercy. Instead, Hana draws herself up, every scarred memory snapping into armor against her skin.

"You come after me again," she says, "I go to the cops. I don't care what you think you have. I don't owe you anything."

He leans back, lips curling wider into a chilling, knowing smile—then stalks out of the alley and into the late-day press of humanity, leaving a seam of cold right down the center of her chest.

Across the street, unseen in the deep blue shadow under a flickering deli awning, Silas watches every shift of Hana's posture, every nervous flick of her hand. He stands motionless, gray eyes tracking her, calculating responses, considering lines not to cross. He wants to move—intervene, crush the threat with a phone call—but he stays rooted, knowing too much interference is its own kind of suffocation. He senses the darkness circling closer: Victor Kane's name on a whispered headline, Selena Voss dangling secrets for leverage, Damian Locke pressing at the city's underbelly. The Brotherhood's enemies sharpen their knives not just for Silas but for anyone who matters to h im.

Hana returns to the café's glow. Her breath is unsteady, hands trembling as she wipes a clean spot on the counter for no reason at all. But her spine is straight, chin tilted higher, eyes all iron and defiance.

Her ex stands under burnt orange light outside, still watching, his gaze searing a warning through the glass. Silas melts into the moving crowd, swept into the city's relentless blur as dusk closes around them all.

Night presses close against the glass of Silas's office, city lights scattered in icy patterns beneath the shadows. The hum of traffic, distant and blurred, pulses through the curved glass, part of the rhythm of his private citadel. Silas stands with a straight spine beside his mahogany desk, a man carved from discipline and dusk, watching Hana where she leans over the far window. She looks small in the moody blue-dark, framed by the lights of Manhattan—a lone figure caught between worlds .

He closes the door with a muted click that seems to echo just a little too long. The air holds a sharpened scent—clean wood, a trace of rare cologne, something metallic beneath it all. Without saying a word, Silas lays the crisp folder on the desk between them. Receipts, bank statements, printed and arranged by the ruthless logic he trusts more than air. His hand lingers on the folder a heartbeat longer than necessary.

"For you," he says, his voice steady, almost too steady. "Your debts. I can end this, Hana. Tonight. My security team...your ex won't bother you again."

Hana's expression fractures. She turns her face away from the glass, shadows sliding over her eyes. Her hand flinches as if from a burn, though no one moves. The folder sits between them like an accusation, pristine and poisonous.

"I don't need you to fix this." Her words sharpen, volume rising above the hush of the city night. She shoves back from the desk before even looking down at the folder. Her palms, pressed to the edge, shake with anger—or is it fear? "You think I want to be a problem for you to solve? I will not be bought off. And I sure as hell don't need your bodyguards swooping in like I'm some broken thing."

Silas's mouth hardens, the lines at the edges of his eyes cutting deeper. He's accustomed to control, to strategies unfolding as intended. Her refusal lands like a blow. The window's reflection shows his own jaw tense, lips flattening as he searches for the right combination of words to break through the wall between them.

"That's not—" His tone quivers just a fraction, gray eyes darkening. "Hana, this isn't about control. I can't stand by while someone threatens you. You have no idea what men like your ex are capable of. This isn't—" He stops, breathes in shallowly. "I lost someone. Once. I swore I'd never watch it happen again."

Her laughter cracks, thin and bitter. "So I'm just the next woman you have to save?" Her eyes shine, not soft, but fierce. "I'm done letting someone else decide what safety means to me. I know exactly what he's capable of. More than you do."

Silas grips the desk, fingers whitening. The city blazes behind him—cold, unreachable, an empire he rules but can never touch. Beneath his immaculate suit, his heart hammers the old, unrelenting story: protection equals love; vigilance means safety. But Hana stands before him, every inch of her radiating the defiance he first admired. It stirs uncomfortable memory—he once saw vulnerability as a wound to cauterize, as a challenge to excise or consume.

"Hana." He says her name like he's trying to keep her in place with the syllables alone. "I learned to protect everything by never letting my guard down. But that's not what this is—" Each word feels like he's prying rusted locks from secrets he's never voiced. "If I could, I'd give you the power to erase him from your life. But if you—if you ask me to step back, I will."

Her mouth twists. "It's not that simple. You think I want to be alone in this? I hate it. But it's mine to handle. If I let you in now, if you make it vanish with a snap and a check...what does that make me? Someone you need to feel needed by? Or just another problem that money can bury?"

Their voices hang in the air, brittle as glass. Silas's face closes, unreadable. But his eyes, pale as morning smoke, betray him. Regret, longing, and a gnawing shame flicker all at once. He wants to reach out, to offer hands that shape destinies, but he hesitates—afraid his touch will only make her small.

Hana folds her arms across her chest, fists clenched tight against her ribs. "I'll handle it. My past, my debts, my mistakes. Maybe that's a line you can't stand not to cross. But if you keep trying, I'll never know if I'm enough on my own."

She pushes away from the desk. The overhead lights dim automatically, shadows slipping over her face, outlining the ghost of fear and pride warring in her silhouette. She doesn't meet his gaze as she storms through the glass door, her steps hard against the silence.

Silas stands alone, the noise of her departure leaving a wound in the charged stillness. The window's panoramic expanse glitters—cold fireworks, a kingdom of glass and stone, utterly indifferent. His hands drop to his sides, useless. He doesn't chase her.

He waits, caught between the urge to break his own rules and the clanging knowledge that the tighter he holds, the more she'll bolt.

Behind his controlled features, frustration knots tight—a king with shattered armor, watching the one thing he can't protect step into the dark.

A bell over the café door lets out a muted chime, but Hana barely hears it in the gentle hush of the morning. Most customers are still curled in their beds, leaving the small corner café bathed in pale light, the air thick with the scent of old books and fresh pastry. Hana sits at the window, her hands wrapped around a cup that's long gone cold, its bitter dregs swirling as she stirs without purpose. Steam from the clatter of the espresso machine drifts, condensing against the glass and blurring the view of a restless city just beyond. Her own reflection stares back: hollow-eyed and knotted with tension.

Amara slides into the seat across from her, coat flaring, clutching a paper bag fragrant with cinnamon. "You barely touched your coffee," she murmurs—gentle, but there's steel beneath it, the kind that takes up space so Hana can breathe.

"It tastes like something scraped from the bottom of a burnt kettle," Hana says, watching the ripples. Humor is armor, but the smile won't come. "Can't complain. It's quiet here."

Amara breaks a piece of pastry, passes it across the table, but her gaze lingers on Hana's trembling fingers. "You want to talk about it?"

"What's there to say?" Hana finally meets her eyes. "I keep thinking I left it behind—him, the debts, the threats. But he's a weed. Every time I think I've pulled up the roots, he's back, growing through the cracks." Her throat tightens, the memory of last night's argument with Silas still raw. "Part of me thinks I have to handle it alone. That letting anyone in just... opens more doors for things to go wrong."

"You're not alone now." Amara's voice is soft, but she leans in, fingertips grazing Hana's sleeve. "Silas—he's not like the others. And you—Hana, you're stronger than you know."

Hana's jaw sets. "That's the problem. He wants to carry everything for me. Pay my debts. Erase my past by writing a check or snapping his fingers. That's not how any of this works. If I let him fix it, I become his project. His responsibility." She shakes her head, the motion sharp. "I can't go backward. I won't be trapped again, even by someone who claims it's for my sake."

"Trust isn't a trap," Amara says. But there's understanding in her eyes—a flicker of her own battles, her own lines drawn. "Sometimes, it's the only way out."

Hana presses her palms to her eyes, her voice small. "What if I'm built for damage? What if every time I trust, all I do is invite disaster in?" The question hangs in the steam and the hush, unanswered.

The city's shadows stretch as morning thickens, and somewhere above the honk and grind of distant traffic, the world tilts toward danger none of them can outrun.

A few blocks uptown, glass towers brood against the predawn gloom. Inside a boardroom stitched together from steel, midnight, and money, Silas stands with his back to the city, gazing out over the lights. Caius reclines at the table, cold blue eyes flicking toward Lucien, whose fingers drum a soundless beat on polished wood.

Silas's voice is razor-sharp, quiet enough to slice tension. "He's in the open now. Contact with Hana last night. Threats. Subtle, for now. That doesn't mean he's acting alone."

Lucien leans forward, the table's reflection splitting his face in half. "You think Victor's moving pieces again?" he asks. "Or is this just a washed-up ex trying his luck?"

They all know Victor Kane's name means poison—smiling through the blood of boardrooms, wielding gossip like a blade. "It's orchestrated," Silas says. "Victor manipulates headlines. Selena Voss stirs up shadows in city hall. Locke's still sniffing at our doors, buying up silence and leverage wherever he can get it."

"All three at once?" Caius snorts. "We've survived them before."

Silas's hand tightens over the back of a leather chair. "We survived because we kept our fractures internal. Now they're looking for weak points. They know about Hana. They'll use her against us if we don't contain this."

For Silas, memory is a battlefield: Victor's cold smile across a negotiating table, Selena's voice dripping false warmth beneath the surface, Damian Locke's threats scribbled on contracts and carried out in alleyways. Each learned where the Brotherhood bled, each carved out a piece. Those scars ache now, warnings of what comes next.

Caius's gaze sharpens. "What's changed?"

"It's not just power or money anymore," Silas says. "It's personal. They want to ruin us, break us open from the inside. Hana is—" His jaw locks. "She's a line I won't let them cross."

By the time the meeting ends, dawn's first light crawls past the city's edge.

Later, Silas sits in a parked car, hands resting on the steering wheel as he stares at Hana's apartment across the street. Through smudged glass, he watches her climb the front steps, arms wrapped tight around herself. It's not a palace or fortress—just a battered door, cracked paint, the kind of place where old ghosts slip through unseen.

He wants to cross the street. He aches to. But the world is tipped now—every move is being watched. If he makes her a target, nothing he does will keep her safe.

Upstairs, Hana finds something shoved under her door—a white envelope, edges dirty where someone's thumb pressed too hard. Inside: a note, all slanted scrawl and venom. Don't trust billionaire saviors. Debts—like secrets—always come due.

Her arms shake, breath hitching as the hallway around her sways in the dim. Below, the city rumbles, indifferent. Outside, Silas waits, eyes burning with promises of war no headline will ever see.

Roses in Ashes

Silas barely speaks as he leads Hana from the cavernous calm of his penthouse living room. Beneath low lamps and the glow of the city steadily devouring twilight through glass, their footsteps land almost soundlessly on the cool stone floors. The doors to the balcony yield with a soft hush, and the chilled air presses gently against their skin. Hana inhales sharply; outside is not just a terrace but an edgeless stage hung above the world, where evening spills in gold and steel blue across faceless towers. Traffic glows and pulses a hundred stories down. The sound is all hush—a wind trembling through glass, distant horns, the city's heartbeat dimmed by height.

Rosy, spectral light bathes the small marble table set close to the railing; on it stands a vase of roses, each flower impossibly vivid—petals black as a raven's wing curled around scarlet hearts. Silas's hand rests on the rail, knuckles white. For a moment, he is silent, scanning the horizon as if searching for an answer painted in the shifting clouds or glinting off the Hudson's knife edge. Hana stands close enough to feel the vibration of him, a thrumming tension that never quite leaves.

"Those," Silas begins, his voice quiet as bruised silk, "were my mother's favorite." He glances at the vase, his usually impassive face showing a flicker of something raw. "She carried a single red rose, always. Even to the hospital. People used to say it was her calling card, as if it meant nothing. But she told me once, 'A rose is both beauty and warning. Love and its thorns.'" His hand lingers near the flowers, hesitant, almost tender.

His mother's memory spills out on the wind now, reluctant and unstoppable. Long ago, their family home was alive with scent—earthy as turned garden beds after summer rain, and that perpetual trace of roses, cloying and sweet, sneaking into linen and walls. His father kept the world at bay with formality and silence; laughter was something secret, whispered among shadows. His mother had been the center—warmth threaded through a cold, watchful house, their Sunday rituals a thousand tiny rebellions against the measured quiet. But loss, when it came, crashed through any pretense of control.

He looks away, eyes flooding with city light. "That last night..." The words grind out, sharp at the edges. "It rained. Hard." The memory grafts itself onto the now—he can almost feel the hospital's sterile chill, the sick fluorescent tremor overhead, the ache in his chest that refused to abate. "She died with a rose on her bedside table. I still smell it sometimes—fresh-cut, almost metallic." For a moment, his fingers shake, a tremor he doesn't bother to hide. "I sat there wanting to bargain with anyone—God, fate, the doctors who wouldn't look me in the eye. It didn't matter. All the power in the world meant nothing."

He doesn't tell Hana about the way his father lingered at the threshold, never crossing fully into grief. Nor how, afterward, life became a series of calculated moves in silent rooms, love rationed out as if it could be spent too quickly. He doesn't mention that his pursuit of strategy—his obsession with secrecy—grew out of shame and helplessness those nights, the impossible wish that if he controlled enough, cared less or more, he might stop that kind of pain from landing again.

The balcony shudders in the rising wind. A distant helicopter cranes overhead, briefly washing them in a pulse of white light, then all is shadow and gold again. Hana reaches for the railing beside him; her hands are careful, uncertain. Her silence is its own comfort, no empty words, no interruption. He feels her gaze on him—steady and gentle, the kind one learns only through earning scars.

The city takes on a strange unreality this high, lights and glass abstracted into something fragile and endless. For Silas, confession is a blade—a risk more dangerous than any rival's blackmail. Victor Kane, his old adversary in the media world, has tried a thousand tricks to worm his way past Silas's walls. So has Selena Voss, all velvet-draped threats and political quicksand, circling for any sign of weakness. Neither has come close to piercing the places Hana stands within now.

In the hush, with roses breathing evening's perfume around them, his armor cracks—just enough. "I've never told that to anyone," he murmurs. "I didn't know I could." His words settle between them like ash, not seeking redemption, just release.

Hana draws nearer, her breaths shallow, her features transforming as she reads the pain behind his calm. She doesn't flinch. Instead, there's something fierce and soft in her jaw, in the heat of her eyes—a silent promise she won't look away from his unraveling, won't mistake his control for distance.

Silas turns away from the city, seeking her face. The balcony is narrow, tucked into the breath of night. All around, the city lights spark awake one by one, indifferent and eternal. For one suspended heartbeat, neither speaks. But in the charged hush, something old and shattering holds—for once, not loneliness, but the fragile possibility of being seen.

Hana leans into the wind, elbows planted on cool glass, the city's reflection bleeding beneath her lowered gaze. Twilight is gone—Manhattan's towers cast a net of hard, glinting lights, and far below, a siren echoes like a wounded animal on the hunt. The marble table's chill seeps through her sleeve. Around her, the hush feels more like a stage set for rupture than comfort. Yet she speaks, her voice barely higher than the rush of air, as if confession might swallow her whole.

"I used to believe loss was a one-time thing," she murmurs, watching a plane etch a vapor trail across the blackening sky. "That after it breaks you, you grow back bone where your heart was." She wraps her fingers together, knuckles paling. "But it sticks, doesn't it? When I lost my sister...it was like the world got smaller, sharper. Since then, every good thing feels...temporary. Like I'm just waiting for it to crack."

She doesn't look at Silas. For a moment, she's no longer Hana Brooks, the woman pieced together from overtime shifts and half-read textbooks, but a girl by a hospital bed, tasting the antiseptic air and the metallic fear that never really faded. She remembers the sound her own heart made: an animal, bristled—waiting to see whether to run or fight.

Wind tugs loose a strand of hair, lashes salt against her cheek. Silence swells beside her. She feels Silas shift—the ghost of movement, expensive wool brushed against the stone. He doesn't offer words, just leans closer, their arms almost touching.

He reaches, his gesture careful, deliberate. His hand finds hers—warm, grounding—and she lets him, surprised at how safety can feel so much like risk. The wind wraps around them, lifting the scent of rain-soaked asphalt and a memory of roses cut through with smoke. From above, the city is all teeth and shimmer, careless to the hearts breaking in its shadows.

Hana's voice trembles as if each word walks a tightrope. "After I left home, it got worse. I thought if I kept moving—new city, new job, new rules—maybe I could outrun it. Then Marcus—my ex—showed me just how wrong I was. When trust goes bad, it's not just heartbreak. It's waking up and not knowing if the person in your bed is ally or predator. What they can take from you. I guess I stopped letting anyone in before they could become a mistake."

Silas's thumb traces a quiet arc against her finger. His silence is not emptiness but attention—he weighs every syllable. For a man who commands rooms, he is oddly patient here, letting pain have its edges.

Their eyes meet. Hana tries for a smile; it comes out crooked. Silas offers his in return—an unpracticed thing, softening the stern lines around his mouth. For a moment, the masks—hers of stubborn defiance, his of unyielding control—shatter, and in the pieces, she glimpses the same brittle longing she keeps chained behind her ribs.

The city sighs beneath them, humming secrets into the dark. The balcony's stone holds the day's warmth, though Hana's heart is a common battlefield—scarred, hopeful, uncertain. She thinks of Silas's story, the ache in his voice as he spoke about his mother, and how his grief mirrors the hollow she's tried to fill by running. Seeing him exposed doesn't cure her fear—if anything, it sharpens it. But it also stirs something fierce and fragile: the hope that maybe two fractured people can carry one another.

Silas shifts his weight, releasing her hand only long enough to reach back for the vase. He plucks a red rose, its petals shadowed and glossy, catching the neon glow that seeps up from the streets. He holds it out, not as a flourish but as an offering—a contract without words.

"For you," he says quietly, his voice low as thunder on the horizon. "This isn't just a reminder of grief. It's living. A promise, not an apology for what's gone."

Hana's breath snags. The rose is heavier than it should be, its stem pressing thorns against her palm—real, anchoring her to now. For once, she doesn't flinch from the sting, doesn't retreat behind sarcasm or steel. Her fingers tremble as she accepts it. She looks up, the city cast in blue and gold behind Silas's silhouette—her world split open, raw and waiting.

"Thank you," she whispers, the words carrying every risk she's spent her life refusing. Below them, the city's pulse beats on—a mosaic of hope and hunger, where trust is a currency more dangerous than anything the world's antagonists—Victor Kane, Selena Voss, Damian Locke—could ever trade in.

Silas just waits. He doesn't let go of her eyes. And in that hush, something fragile and nearly new glimmers between them, hanging above the city that made and nearly broke them both.

Night has settled into the city—a river of diamonds and gold thrown across the asphalt veins of Manhattan, the towers blooming with light far below. The glass doors behind them hush closed, so all that's left is the breeze moving between the two figures on the penthouse balcony, coaxing rose petals to tremble in Hana's hand. Silas stands before her, his gaze both a barrier and a question, a current holding steady as the world rushes beneath.

He barely breathes, searching her face. One hand rises, hovering close, and his eyes are darker in the shadow—their storm concealed, not by intention, but by history that lingers in every careful inch he allows himself to move. Slowly, he leans in, achingly deliberate, stopping just short of her lips. Silas's hand hovers near her cheek, uncertain, as if wrestling with the urge to take or to wait.

He waits. Hana's pulse is a thrumming ache, pressed against her throat and fingertips. Her fingers, still curled around the stem of the rose, tighten and release as she takes in the man before her: the strategist brought low by the memory of old grief, the architect of secrets daring to pause for something as fragile as hope. Her breath catches—half uncertainty, half longing—and it is she who draws that sliver of distance closed.

The kiss is not hungry. It's gentle but not safe, blooming between them in slow increments—a question, an answer, the balancing of sorrow and trembling desire. Silas's hand cups the line of Hana's jaw, his fingers calloused but careful, anchoring her in the moment as dusk concedes to night. City air, scented faintly with rain and the far-off memory of roses, presses silently against their skin.

When they part, the world does not reclaim its usual noise. Only a hush remains on the balcony, caught between them like a breath neither is willing to let go. Their foreheads rest together, skin to skin, and their hands—hers entwined with his, the dewy rose cupped gently between them—act as a shield against all the brokenness outside this private world. Silas closes his eyes, a ragged exhale betraying the tension he holds even now. Hana's lashes flutter, her half-smile uncertain.

"I still can't believe you're real," Silas murmurs, the words carrying none of his usual reserve.

Hana's reply is soft, the kind of honesty she has rarely allowed herself. "It feels like we're somewhere else. Like the world can't touch us here."

He lets out a hollow, weary sound—almost laughter, almost grief. "It always touches us, Hana. Out there...it never stops. But I can try to give us this."

She presses her hand over his—a silent promise, shared in shadows. "I'm tired of running. Tired of being afraid."

His hand tightens on hers for a moment, as if to chase away the ghosts—enemies with names, cane-wielding media titans like Victor Kane, the political predator Selena Voss who hungers for every Brotherhood weakness, and the serpent Damian Locke, always waiting for another's slip.

For an instant, Hana lets the city fall away. The skyline, with its neon shimmer, is a living thing—alive, humming, embodying both peril and promise. She tastes the metallic chill of the wind and the bittersweet tang of memory. Her scars, normally hidden beneath cuff and sleeve, seem to thrum with fresh awareness. Here is Silas, stripped of armor, closing his eyes beneath the cathedral darkness, opening himself not with grand confession but with proximity—a wordless yielding.

She senses the shift between them—a trembling bridge forged by raw honesty. It isn't resolution. It is the hush at the center of the storm, that moment neither escape nor surrender. And Hana, bracing herself on the cool marble rail, realizes with a clarity knife-sharp and sudden: here is her choice. The line she draws in the ash.

She could step back. Let distance do what fear always craves. Or she could choose this: the risk of heartbreak, the possibility of something unruined. Silas's face is inches from hers, his jaw tight with restraint, eyes open now and searching hers for a sign, a verdict—anything to anchor him as the city threatens to pull him under.

"I want to fight for this," Hana says, her voice just above a whisper, present for only the balcony and the man who lingers before her. "I can't promise it'll be easy."

"No one can," Silas replies, his voice rough—vulnerable in the way that means more than any oath. "But I won't let go. Not if you stay."

She nods, swallowing the last shards of hesitation. The glimmer from thousands of windows paints her skin with gold and silver. The rose in her hand becomes more than a symbol of mourning or warning; it is a red pulse in the dark, alive with color and meaning she hasn't dared to claim before.

Together, they stand in the hush, her fingers laced with his, watching hope bloom quietly in the night. Hana does not know if the city will ever be safe, or if love will weather the storms that still gather. But the choice is hers now—a promise, a beginning. And for tonight, that is enough.

The Breaking Point

The corridors of Silas Carver's media tower are silent at midnight—no voices echo along the marble floors, only the steady hum of servers deep behind glass. On the uppermost floor, all that marks Hana Brooks's arrival is the faint scuff of her sneaker soles. She steps beneath the soft, calculated glow reserved for titans and ghosts. The aftertaste of bitter espresso lingers on her tongue; she remembers his smile from hours earlier. She holds onto that memory, her knuckles tight around a borrowed lanyard that she tucks into her pocket as she slips inside the private office.

Mahogany, steel, charcoal blue—the room thrums with power and quiet judgment. Silas's scent clings to the air: cedar and cold spice, darker now against the filtered light of Midtown's neon skyline. Rows of books stand like sentinels behind glass, and tucked among them is a single red orchid, almost blood-black against its white vase. Hana inhales, braving the hush.

She crosses to the desk, her legs trembling. Her fingers hover over the terminal, watching streetlights blink like dying stars outside the window. Shadows from skyscrapers stretch long over the city. She settles into his leather chair—an intimacy that feels as sharp as trespass.

The screens wake at her touch, the glass pure beneath her palm. The password—she'd watched him type those deft keys three nights ago, silent as a cat, half ashamed at how easily curiosity overpowers her better sense. Her breath stutters as she enters the string—his mother's favorite painting, the one he told her about between confessions.

The machine unlocks.

Below surface folders—finance charts, dry forecasts, Brotherhood minutes—there's a ghost directory hidden lower than the rest: Contingency Operations. A click.

Her heart ticks. She scrolls through cold blueprints for campaigns and timelines, each marked with precision. And then, the name: Victor Kane. Hana knows the stories about Victor—rival media king, rumor of the century, the sort of man who collects enemies the way Silas collects secrets.

The files bare themselves with a clinical violence. On-screen, Hana sees email chains marked URGENT, layouts for media strikes, draft headlines dripping venom: "Kane's Empire Built on Lies"—"Investigative Report: Victor Kane's Shadow Syndicates."

She reads correspondence. Each directive flows from Silas—the soft, careful man she's kissed, exposed in these clipped commands.

"Run with the allegations. Source: anonymous. Timeslot, Wednesday at ten. Pair with market drop."

"Coordinate with the political desk. Leak by midnight. Keep Cain out of it. My approval required."

And always, after each chain, Silas's digital signature—unmistakable, stamped with chilling finality.

Hana's hands start shaking. Is this what power looks like? Is this how media empires are made—by binding truth and rumor together with silk and barbed wire?

A document blinks, and she prints it, the ancient scent of scorched toner tickling her nose. The paper is warm and fragile as breath. In the lamplight, words sharpen into accusations, lines dissecting Victor Kane's life, career, and private habits—facts and fictions bleeding together at Silas's instruction.

Her pulse thunders inside her ears.

She sits back, letting the cold city fill her vision. Manhattan sprawls below, bright and eternal. Hana sees her own ghost in the glass, wide-eyed and stunned, city light fracturing across her skin. She remembers only hours ago—the warmth in his voice, the softness nestled under his wounds, his hand steady on hers, and a promise hovering unspoken in the dark. Now, betrayal sours her mouth.

Her thoughts twist. Who is Silas Carver when no one is left to witness? When he leans in to murmur comfort, is that just the mask, or is the mask the man she's reading here?

She wants to slam the files shut, to believe none of it, to go back to whispered confessions on the balcony where he'd bared a piece of himself no one else saw. But the hard truth gleams from the documents—justice rewritten for victory, trust bent to the will of the Brotherhood, lives like Victor Kane's measured out for destruction if necessary.

If she confronts him, what happens to them then?

If she says nothing, is she complicit—or just another pawn on the board, gilded and dispensable?

She stares at Silas's signature and feels the old bruise of betrayal stirring—a memory of broken promises and debts she'd fought so hard to escape.

In the distance, somewhere below, a siren wails and dies on the avenue. The scent of Manhattan—electric rain on asphalt, oil, sweat, hope—seeps through the glass. She edges forward: gathering the papers, aligning each damning page, every move meticulous and deliberate. Her right hand trembles as she tucks the documents into her bag.

The pulse of the city will not slow for scandal or heartbreak.

Hana rises, closes the folder, and smooths trembling fingers along the mahogany edge. Time slows as her reflection wavers in the window—a woman caught between compassion and cold arithmetic.

The click of the office door as she exits is almost silent. Hana leaves with her secret, a promise burning between her ribs. She will not run. She will find Silas Carver. And this time, she will demand the truth.

The faint chime of the elevator cuts through the hush as Hana steps out, her arms stiff around her chest. The penthouse foyer swallows her in shadows; only the city's scattered neon—red, blue, a jealous green—casts trembling specters through beveled glass. Her jaw is set, her eyes raw, and the clutch of pages in her hand trembles with every ragged breath. The floor beneath her shoes, polished obsidian, feels unnervingly cold. She calls out, her voice faltering on the first syllable.

"Silas?"

A soft click. A silhouette emerges near the window, nearly camouflaged against the gloom. Silas's back is rigid, his suit jacket thrown over his shoulders as though he never left work, the faintest silver at his temples catching stray light. Glass clinks against the mahogany ledge as he sets down a lowball he hasn't sipped from.

He turns, his eyes scanning her with a strategist's focus—sharp, dissecting, but slow to reveal worry.

"You shouldn't be here this late." His words run low, deliberate, clipped as if rationed. "What's wrong?"

Stillness grips the air. Hana crosses the expanse—city lights smearing across her face, her breath coming fast and shallow. She thrusts the documents against his chest, the motion punctuated by a rasp of paper. The room smells faintly of cedar and a lingering, sharp tang of gin.

"I found these," she breathes, her voice knife-edged. "I know what's in them, Silas. The attack on Victor Kane—all those stories you ordered... when did you decide you could ruin people and just sign your name at the bottom? Did you ever ask yourself if it was right?"

He takes the pages. Not a flinch, not a hitch in the movement—but his other hand flexes open, then clenches on nothing. He barely glances at the first sheet before stacking them methodically on the table beside the decanter. When he finally answers, the chill in his voice is measured, calculated to contain—yet behind it, something brittle threatens to snap.

"Sometimes, to keep the Brotherhood safe, there are lines I have to cross—lines you'd never imagine. Victor Kane is not just a rival. Men like him, Selena Voss, Damian Locke—they'd see us destroyed. If I hesitate, they don't. And there's more at stake than my own conscience."

A muted rumble of distant traffic creeps through double-pane glass. Hana's shoulders round forward, her outline hardening against the blue glow from the city below. Paper rattles as her hands tremble, fury flaring in the set of her jaw even as her eyes glisten. The silence stretches. Heat from her accusation and the cold from his answer hang in a perfect, agonizing equilibrium.

"How can you live like this?" She paces before the panoramic window, her reflection and his mingling in the glass—two ghosts divided by the empty room. Her fingers dig crescents into her palms. "You approve lies—ruin careers—just for leverage. For what? To keep your empire safe? What about the people who get crushed beneath all your moves?"

A hollow laugh gropes its way from her throat, nearly drowned by the city's far-off sirens. "Is this who you are, Silas? Or just the part you let me see tonight?"

His hands drop to his sides, rigid, as he's caught in the pale corridor between window and world. For an instant, the steel in his posture fades, the mask slipping at the edges.

"You think I wanted you in this?" His voice fractures, rough tinder beneath the words. "You were never supposed to find what I bury for everyone else. But you're here now, and I can't shield you from what this life demands. You wanted the truth, Hana. Here it is: My world asks for loyalty that costs everything. There's no room for innocence. Only survivors."

She swallows, the taste of copper on her tongue, a metallic echo of trust burnt away. Her feet still, the city's radiance painting her profile in fractured color. Her chest rises and falls; but every intention, every argument that might have built a bridge between them scatters on the marble like shattered glass.

He's a shadow, divided—his reflection fractured, real form and mirrored self cleaved by the darkness that lies between.

Silence deepens. Outside, the traffic signals blink. A siren fades; laughter drifts up from a rooftop party far below. Within the penthouse, the only movement is Hana's shoulders as she turns away—hunched, defeated, every line of her frame spelling loss that language can't touch. Across the gulf of polished black stone, Silas stands rooted. The city hums, oblivious, as the chasm between them yawns wide, and neither reaches across.

Hana slips from the penthouse before the city's sunrise can catch her with tear-streaked cheeks. Manhattan feels almost alien at this hour; the golden hush of dawn is swallowed by the sterile hum of power beneath steel and glass. She ignores Silas's offer—his voice thin as retreating footsteps—and heads into the tangle of streets, her coat wrapped tighter with each step. The wind needles through wool, biting at her ankles. Each stride is a desperate command: don't look back.

Her boots echo against the concrete canyons, drowned by distant horns and the sizzle of streetlights flickering awake. Above her, skyscrapers press in—cold titans, no comfort in their grandeur. With every block, Hana finds herself cataloging betrayals as if tallying scars on her body: her ex's threats, the suffocating debts, the cruel games of men in glass offices. Silas's name knots in her throat. He was supposed to be different. But the chill seeping through her sleeves matches the ache blooming through her chest.

Days pass. Hana pours herself into work at the Greenwich café, each shift a blur of clattering plates and the cloying scent of espresso and burnt sugar. At closing, the city's neon script crawls across frosted windows, painting her in light and shadow. Her phone buzzes—a name she can't delete—so she stuffs it deep in her bag until silence reigns again. Coworkers share sly looks, offering sympathy laced with curiosity she refuses to feed.

She shuffles pastries, wipes down tables, and loses herself in the familiar rhythm: orders, laughter, the constant shuffle of customers. But in the pocketed quiet between shifts, her mind circles the same impossible questions. Was any of it—any of him—real? Had Silas known she'd see that side of him, the one who weaponized stories and ruined lives for power's sake? Had he wanted her to, in some twisted way?

Sleep is another battleground. Every time she closes her eyes, the city's din presses against the glass. Memory twists: the softness in Silas's eyes when night fell, his hand trembling against hers on the balcony. Now all warmth is tarnished. His digital signature burns at the bottom of those documents—cold, irrevocable proof. Victor Kane—his rival, Manhattan's other phantom king—just another casualty in Silas's private war. Betrayal in a language of headlines and ruined reputations.

And miles away, Silas turns himself into a machine. His corner office is a museum of vacuumed carpets and humming servers. He stacks meetings against the night; each one an armor plate, every decision a layer of insulation against the guilt gnawing at his core. Colleagues tread lightly—whispering when he storms past. Silas responds with clipped commands, his eyes fixed on the glowing skyline. No one dares pierce the perimeter he builds around himself. He works until the city blurs from blue dusk into sickly electric morning, leaving nothing but exhaustion and ghosts behind his tired eyes.

They collide days later in a crowded elevator—a moment stretched on the knife's edge. Hana is pressed between strangers, the air heavy with perfume and stale anxiety. The doors part. She lifts her gaze to meet his: Silas, angular in his shadowed suit, jaw set, lashes casting tiny, trembling crescents on his cheekbones. For a heartbeat, something almost cracks. Then Hana looks away, her fingers white-knuckled on the handrail. Silas doesn't move or speak. The air between them coils with everything unspoken, everything irreparably changed.

That night, Hana stands at her window in the yellow hush of her small apartment, her hands braced on the cold sill. The city stretches out—a maze of promises and betrayals dressed in glittering midnight.

Out there, stories are currency, and monsters look just like men in pressed suits. She lets her forehead rest against the frigid pane. Her reflection is a ghost—tired eyes, lips bitten raw. Who am I now, with these secrets under my skin, with trust gone brittle?

She remembers how she used to imagine happiness as simple: a warm touch, laughter softening the edges of the day. Now every hope carries a shadow—what if love is simply another lie, another layer to strip away until nothing remains? She aches to believe the tenderness she'd shared with Silas meant something, that some small part of him had been real beneath the calculated darkness. She wonders if trust can ever grow back from scorched earth—or if longing will always outlive forgiveness.

The city watches, glittering and indifferent, through glass that won't yield. Hana closes her eyes, letting the sounds of Manhattan bleed through: a siren, the hush of passing tires, a distant belt of laughter. Somewhere, Silas sits alone in his sterile fortress of light, every wall thick with secrets, every window reflecting the man he's chosen to become. And still, Hana can't let go of the small, stubborn hope that one day the world might look softer again.

But for now, she just stands there, breathing the cold, her longing blooming in the dark.

Giving In

S ilas ushers Hana through the penthouse door, the hush of midnight echoing in the deep marble foyer. He barely glances at her, but his hand gestures—precise, deliberate—invite her further in. The city sprawls outside, blinding and endless through glass; Manhattan glitters, full of cunning reflections, as if every window is watching their every move.

He flicks a dimmer switch, sinking the room into a cocoon of low gold and moody blue. Shadows gather under the arms of velvet sofas and pool along the base of blackened wood. Hana slides quietly onto the deep crimson couch, hugging her knees. The air inside carries a hint of spiced bourbon and old paper, overlaying the faint floral notes of her perfume.

Silas stands apart, his posture rigid as iron. He drifts to the panoramic window, pacing—visible in the glow, but not in the details, a man outlined against all of Manhattan. His fingers tap the glass. Steam coats his breath; his silhouette vibrates ever so slightly.

"Do you ever wonder," he says, his voice almost swallowed by the hum of the city, "if there's anywhere left in the world that's truly safe? With enough money, you imagine nothing can actually hurt you. It's a lie. Even at the top, you can never buy yourself out of danger. Or fear." His words move through the air, brittle as frost.

He turns, letting the city's lights sculpt the hollows beneath his cheekbones. For once, his expression is unguarded, exhausted. There's a flicker in his steely eyes—something haunted, ancient, desperate not to be revealed.

"I built this place to be a fortress," he confesses, his voice lower. "But I can't make it a sanctuary." He lets a bitter smile twist the scar on his jaw. "Control is a mask. One I wear because I don't know how to do anything else. Because if I take it off, everything I care about might collapse."

He crosses the expanse in measured steps. Each one is silent, but the tension hangs heavy—an animal coiled in the heart of the room. His destination is a mahogany bookshelf that stretches across one wall like the spine of an old beast. He doesn't search; his fingers find a battered volume by instinct. Its cloth cover is frayed, the letters worn away—something from another life.

He holds the book out but doesn't open it. "I was seven when my mother died." The words trickle out, almost reluctant. "She was the only person who could quiet the storms in my father or me. Her funeral was the first time I realized that not even the richest, most powerful people in Manhattan could keep tragedy out." His gaze falters; he runs a thumb over the spine, exhaling shakily. "It's strange, what you keep. This book—her hands once turned these pages at night. I still remember the smell—rosewater and tobacco—her voice in the dark, promising that monsters were only stories."

His knuckles whiten on the book. "She lied. The monsters are real. They just wear better suits now—smile for headlines, shake hands in empty boardrooms. Like Victor Kane. Like Selena Voss—waiting for any fracture in the Brotherhood to break us all. They circle beneath the glass and steel, always hungry."

He swallows. The memory is sharp, a wound pressed raw. He holds the book to his chest a heartbeat longer, then sets it reverently on the marble table, a talisman against memories he can't erase.

Crossing back to Hana, he sits on the sofa's edge—close, but not quite touching. His suit jacket is gone, sleeves rolled to his forearms. There's something naked in the way he holds himself, in the way he stares at the skyline instead of at her. Finally, he turns.

"If you stay here," he murmurs, "if you stay with me—there's a chance you'll get hurt. Not just by men like Kane, by my enemies. By me." His voice drops, rough around the edges. "I don't trust myself not to ruin things I care about—because I have before. I am afraid. Of what I've done in the Brotherhood's name. Of what I might still have to do. But mostly, I am afraid of losing you—before I ever really have y ou."

He takes her hand, lifting it with reverence, setting it flat over his heart. The thud beneath her palm is unsteady, nothing like the calm strategist the world believes him to be. He doesn't speak. They sit, joined only by desperate silence, the pulse of blood and music in the background.

Silas's internal walls buckle, the fortress becoming a glass house at last. He leans in, his forehead resting against Hana's, their breaths mingling. The city fades, leaving only the fragile darkness between the two of them—where, for a single moment, neither power nor fear holds sway, and even grief softens in the gentle exchange of vulner- ability.

The city hangs outside Silas's penthouse like a suspended fever dream, cobalt and gold rippling through the glass as if Manhattan itself were holding its breath. The living room is dim—soft, shadowed lamplight kissing the edge of the black velvet sofa where Hana sits, her shoulders tight, fists pressed into the cushions as if she might keep herself from floating away. The muted thrum of a piano track drifts through hidden speakers, filling the gaps that tension cannot reach.

Silas leans into the hush, his elbows poised on his knees, eyes fixed on the skyline. Hana watches the way he's been unraveling, thread by careful thread—she feels each note of his rare honesty still vibrating in the air between them. It stirs something raw in her, exposing how close she is to fleeing. And yet, she doesn't. Her own reflection gleams faintly in the window behind him: small, determined, frightened.

She draws a slow, uncertain breath, scooting closer so her knee almost grazes his. Her hands tremble, betraying every ounce of courage she has scraped together for this. All night, words have built inside her throat: jagged, peeled back, impossible to swallow. This is the risk—the line between burning and blooming that she has danced along for so long.

"I'm scared, Silas," she says, her voice carving through the quiet. "Not of you. Of what you mean to me. Every step I take here, with you—it's like walking into fire and hope at the same time. I never know which one's going to win."

She stares at the rings her hand leaves on her jeans, the traces of her anxiety laid bare. Her heart throbs wildly, caught between the echo of past hurts and the fragile chance of more.

Silas's posture shifts, minutely—his gaze pulling from the city to her face, as if he's reading bruises that aren't visible, scars beneath her skin. He says nothing. It is his silence that allows her to go on.

Hana's body curls inward as old memories drag at her. She looks down, letting her hair fall forward to catch the sting in her eyes. "I keep thinking about the night I realized my ex was lying to me." Her voice cracks, barely audible. "He left me with nothing but a pile of debt and a promise that it was all my fault. Some nights, I still lie awake and count every dollar I owe—like if I reach the number, I'll find a way out. But I never do. I just get stuck."

Her chin lifts, just enough to meet Silas's haunting, storm-grey stare. It's the first time she's truly looked at him since their voices last clashed, since angry words cracked trust and left it splintered between them. She doesn't flinch.

"I want to say I'm stronger now, but every instinct tells me to run. From you. From all of this." Her confession hangs, brittle as frost.

Another stillness. The city lights behind Silas seem to pulse, refracting hope and hesitation onto the planes of his face. He watches her as someone gazing out over thin ice, uncertain if the next step will hold or break.

Hana's shoulders buck as she draws in a shaky breath. "Except... you're not like them." Her words fall quietly, uncertainly. "There's something in you—maybe it's your brokenness, or the way you admit you're afraid. I can see it. You make me want to stay, even when I know what it could cost."

She shifts, pressing her head to his shoulder. The fabric of his shirt is cool beneath her cheek, a barrier and a balm. Though his body is tense, the nearness is real—the warm thump of his heart, the faint scent of bitter citrus and old paper, the iron tang of his world unspooling against hope.

"I want to trust you," she whispers, more to herself than to him. "Even when everything I've survived tells me not to."

Silas tilts his hand, careful, and she fits her trembling fingers inside his. Hana's skin feels feverish—nerves singing of risk and relief as she lets herself linger in the touch. She's too raw to hide, too tired of pushing everyone away, her tears spilling silent and hot. She shakes, but this time—she doesn't pull back.

Outside, a siren blurs by, its wail a phantom that never quite reaches them. Here, in their shadowed cocoon, Hana lets the weight fall away. She breathes in, her mouth trembling, afraid she might shatter entirely if she moves. But she doesn't. Instead, she turns her face—slow, deliberate—and presses her lips, featherlight, to the scar on Silas's jaw.

They don't speak. The moment stretches long and breathless, trust growing like the first fragile roots through scorched earth.

Some wounds are too deep for words. But tonight, the city lights bear witness as two souls—bruised but unbroken—risk belonging to each other.

Silas leads Hana down the marble-floored corridor, the only light a faint electric blue drifting from under the bedroom door, a promise of sanctuary in the watchful dark. Their hands stay welded together, their shadows fractured against the glass as they cross the threshold. He pauses there—shoulders drawn, as if the city sprawled at his back weighs heavier than usual tonight. The hum of the penthouse softens to the sigh of distant traffic. Something unspoken flickers in his eyes as he looks at Hana: a solemn promise, or maybe the simplest plea for forgiveness. He draws her close, pressing his lips to hers—slow, deep, the kiss long outlasting their first frantic heartbeat, each silent second stretching the air between them into something breathless.

She presses in, unmoored. The world recedes, leaving only the shapes and sighs of their bodies slotted together in the cool, darkened room. Silas's hands come to rest on Hana's waist—gentle, reverent, as if he's afraid she might vanish should he hold her too tightly. Hana answers in kind, lacing her arms around his neck, holding him as though anchoring herself through a storm. As the city spins indifferently beyond the windows, their embrace becomes more than desire—desperate, yes, but sacred, too. The invisible walls they've kept built for years, chipped and bruised by betrayals neither of them voice, begin to dissolve. His mouth finds her jaw, brushes the scar she once hid from every mirror, and she drags in a shaky breath that tastes of salt and skin and the faint copper in the night air.

Sheets cool as rainwater gather beneath their tangled limbs. The Manhattan skyline glitters in slivers between the swaying drapes—a net of gold to catch their falling hearts. Silas's voice is almost too soft to hear, confession pressed into Hana's skin in a chain of broken sentences.

"I'm sorry—for every time I pushed you away."

Fingertips brush the arch of her back, trembling slightly, a man unused to apologies, now desperate to make them. "For the secrets. For the weight I put on you."

His words are as raw as open wounds, apologies bleeding into promises. "I never meant for you to carry my darkness. I never wanted you hurt." He buries his face in the hollow of her throat.

Her laughter, soft and genuine—a sound he's learned to crave, an antidote to the silence he's cultivated. Hana answers not with questions or blame, but with the press of her palm over his heart, her breath warm along his temple.

"I know. I know, Silas." It comes out as a tremulous whisper, equal parts reassurance and surrender. "You don't have to wear the whole world tonight. Just let me... let me be enough for you, here."

Her hands are butterflies over knotted muscle, tracing the history of loss written in the scars across his chest. She murmurs secrets of her own: pieces of her old life, the betrayal that stung so deep it nearly hollowed her out. She speaks of debts, of long nights in the city when loneliness gnawed through her defenses. Against his skin, the words feel less like confessions and more like offerings—vulnerabilities laid out like cracked stones, before the night might tumble them away.

Between them, gravity shifts. Words dry up. Their dialogue becomes the rustle and wrack of limbs, the gentle collision of laughter and tears. Her nails scrape gently at his scalp, urging away the thoughts of enemies perched in offices high above, of Victor Kane's sharpened vengeance and Selena Voss's whispered threats.

"Don't let them take this from you, Silas. Not tonight. Not ever."

He lifts his head, meeting her gaze in the near-dark. "You're the only thing that's real. The only thing that's mine."

She smiles, and it's like sunrise finding the ruined corners of his soul.

He presses her closer. They dance through the hours: whispers tangled with sighs, tender as prayer, fierce as survival. Time curls around the swell of desire and the hush of exhausted limbs. The city's pulse slows to the rhythm of their breathing. Silas learns her laughter in the dark, the taste of her forgiveness—bitter and sweet. Hana learns that his shuddering apologies aren't just guilt, but a plea for salvation neither dared seek.

Dawn slants in peach and pewter through the glass. The storm of the night has passed, not erased but remade. Hana curls against Silas, her leg thrown over his, tracing thoughtless circles on his arm while outside, danger sharpens its teeth but dares not breach this thin-walled oasis. He presses his lips to her knuckles, memorizing the softness, the ache of hope that lingers between them.

Neither speaks. The words have finally run out—every secret, every fear spent and tangled in the sheets as the city wakes beyond the window. They hold each other in the hush, knowing with absolute certainty this night has changed everything.

Even as the world sharpens outside—rival empires stirring, old enemies tracing their names in ash and ambition—here, inside this bloodred dawn, trust is fragile, binding, and new. Neither one dares let go.

The Secret

Night presses down on Silas's penthouse, folding the city into its secrets. The study waits in charcoal stillness, recessed lights faint behind smoked glass. Hana slips in. Every step hushes against the Persian rug, her heart thudding a nervous tattoo in her wrist. The skyline stares back—glass and steel gleaming in indigo, Manhattan whispering stories she wishes she could tune out. A reflection flickers in the window, her own face haloed by light. She draws in a shaky breath and turns to the desk.

She has never actually sat here. The mahogany is cold beneath her palms, wide enough to swallow her small frame, littered with stark order: a black notebook, a smooth obsidian pen, and a single white rose in a low vase, browning at the edges. A scent of expensive paper and orchid soil—sharp, secretive—clings to the air.

She kneels, fingers groping beneath the bottom drawer until they brush the catch Silas used the night before. The compartment clicks open. An encrypted drive, anonymous, innocuous. Her hands are steady—she trained them to be, working café shifts through chaos, fixing ancient espresso machines with trembling nerves—but her breath shivers anyway as she slots the drive into his terminal.

The screen pulses to life. Password prompt. Her mind flicks back to last night: Silas, silhouetted by moonlight, murmuring numbers to himself as he keyed them in. Hana keys them in now, hears the subtle whir of hidden engines spinning, and feels the room's gravity lock. Layers of security unfold before her like a series of locked doors—hints of who Silas is, truly, scrolling past her eyes. She slips through each one, the forbidden password on her lips like a prayer she doesn't dare finish.

A new folder winks in the file system, stamped with the old constellation: The Orion Brotherhood, empire of secrecy. She double-clicks. Digital progress bars crawl, neon green against midnight blue. Files begin to flow—a torrent, not a trickle. In this hush, every loading beep could be an alarm about to wail.

The documents are organized with chilling precision. Wire transfer spreadsheets. PDF after PDF: legal bribes masked as philanthropy, hospital invoices and silent settlements, names of doctors and politicians she has never met. Each log links back to the names she has heard in guarded conversations—Victor Kane, king of media rivals; Damian Locke, predator in a suit; Selena Voss, the ice-queen politician with a phoenix on her wrist. Even incidents Hana didn't know existed, cover-ups from years past, details that shouldn't exist. She scrolls, scrolling faster.

One file glows brighter than the others: "For Destruction Only."

Her breath stalls. For a moment, she wonders if she should look away, wheeling her chair from the screen. But control is a mirage, and this is the moment that decides everything. She double-clicks.

Silas's voice emerges from the penthouse sound system—measured and low, as intimate as a confession, as clinical as a eulogy.

"...we neutralize Caius Drake's investment rival through a fake insider-trading leak—make it untraceable, understood? Lucien will tie up legal ends. Darius's hospital scandals: contained, for now. Orion, we reroute digital forensics. Victor Kane must not see it coming. Kane is volatile—I want Locke's firm tied up in regulatory shadowplay. Voss's leverage is weakened; if it's exposed, the Brotherhood survives, but no one walks away clean. Above all, torch the backups. Do it, or don't call yourself my ally."

Silas's voice doesn't tremble. There is no warmth or regret. Just clarity. The very same control she saw in the gentle lines of his hand, tracing the edge of her jaw that morning, now repurposed as a weapon, as a blueprint for survival and ruin.

Hana's pulse races, veins aching. She rounds her shoulders, staring through layers of words—each line of strategy, each ruthless instruction. Somewhere in that voice, she tries to find the man who smiled, almost shy, over coffee; the man who let her glimpse vulnerability when the city was sleeping. But his voice is a glacier, unyielding, and she shivers.

The files bloom beneath her cursor: charts of payoffs, maps of secret backdoors into rival servers, notes of surveillance—on enemies, on allies, on anyone who might one day matter. Emails from the Brotherhood's four. Not just business—personal threats cataloged, marriages stitched together with silence, blackmail arranged with mathematical detachment.

All the while, the city pulses below. If these files ruptured, what would Manhattan look like at dawn? Scandal, exposure, the Brotherhood burning from its marble roots—Silas and his brothers, all ashes. She sees Victor's name, Kane's threats—recalls whispered mentions. Power, always negotiated in darkness.

What is trust in a world built on secrets? She is nothing more than collateral damage now, swept up in the same current that forged and fractured him. Was she ever safe?

Her hand rises, slow, and covers her mouth. The computer's blue glow paints her features ghostly. Every word on the screen opens a wider chasm inside her. Silas's final words echo, chilling the hollow of her chest:

"If the light hits these shadows, we all burn."

The penthouse hush closes around her. Hana stares, faith splintering. She cannot look away, not even as her heart begins to break.

Printer light flickers, casting a cold, clinical glow across the ink-scented air of Silas's study. Page after page stacks in a neat, damning pile—a slow mechanical rhythm that jars in this hush, each fresh sheet stark with secrets. Hana's fingers tremble as she lifts the first document. The paper edges bite. She counts the evidence: page after page, each one heavier than the last. Her jaw quivers. The taste of copper regret lingers from where she has bitten her lip. She doesn't let herself read just yet, not fully—just lets the weight settle in her arms, lets the gravity of what she has uncovered drag her to the edge.

Behind her, the city glares through the curtainless glass—midnight high-rises afloat in smog and moonlight. Across the room, the velvet sofa calls, crimson cushions glowing beneath the sallow gaze of the rose painting, its saturated petals bursting out of black like hope struggling against rot. Hana sits, papers pressed to her heart, eyes burning as tears carve silent tracks down her cheeks. Each word, each number—wire transfers, incident reports, code names—buzzes in her mind in sick, telescoping lines. The city's hum seeps into the silence, an indifferent lullaby.

She tries to breathe slowly, but the air tastes strange—cloying with the scent of expensive leather, stale single malt, and his aftershave: basil, smoke, secrets. The stack shakes in her grip.

Images surface, severing the present. She sees Silas's hand tangled with hers over coffee, his thumb tracing the hollow between her knuckles, steadying her while the world outside trembled with storm. She sees him in the kitchen, moon-limned and soft-mouthed, his lips pressed to her temple with a gentleness she had thought rare, maybe even holy. She sees him smile—truly smile, not the strategic curl he wears for adversaries but the kind that cracks his shield for one wild, unguarded instant. Each memory collides with these printouts—wire transfers signed in his hand, strategy memos cold with legalese. Laughter is replaced by allegations, kindness by calculated ruin. Pages blur; she blinks, tears pricking sharp as needles.

She never imagined loving someone could feel like freefall. Or that landing could be such violence.

In the hush, her voice fractures:

"Who are you?"

She is not talking to the empty room, not really. The question hangs between velvet and marble and glass. Somewhere, beneath her skin, her pulse stutters—anger and heartbreak tangling. Another whisper, choked raw.

"How could you do this? To them. To me?"

She waits, as if the city's pulse, the bloodbeat in her ears, the spectral face in the painting, might offer an answer. But no reply comes—not from Silas, not from the city, not from the blood-red rose whose petals fall in silence.

She slumps deeper into the velvet, clutching the ignoble truths close as shield and wound alike. The chill of the room finds her bones, settles there like winter never left. A sound, nearly animal, escapes her chest—half sob, half gasp, as if she has dropped something vital and can't find the shape to retrieve it. Betrayal isn't a cut; it's a hollowing, a sickness that seeps and stains. Her shoulders shake with it.

She tries to remember the texture of Silas's voice—warm, amused, wounded, alive. But all she hears now is the measured, silken cadence of his schemes from the hidden file, naming Caius, Lucien, Darius, Orion, explaining how to turn friends into shields and enemies into shadows. Victor Kane, Damian Locke, those names inked into every corridor of the scandal—rivals, yes, but also victims of games played on a scale she never dreamed.

If there's a storybook world where trust isn't a currency and love isn't weaponized, Hana can't see the path there now. Maybe, she muses, in some mirror universe, Silas would have chosen her over Brotherhood, over legacy, over vengeance and ruthlessness. In that kinder world, his arms would mean haven instead of hazard. But that place is as unreachable as the backside of the moon. Here, reality is steel and marble, midnight and ashes.

She wonders, dazed—if he could lie so perfectly, so tenderly, was anything hers? Did she ever touch the real man, or just a figure in the labyrinth of his own making? Was every intimacy a carefully drawn trap, every confession mapped with the precision of a chess player pocketing pieces for a final move?

She presses the papers to her chest. Their corners scrape her skin, anchoring her to what's left. Hope dissolves, molecule by molecule, replaced with panic, then with the resigned ache of someone finding herself utterly, dangerously alone.

For a moment, she imagines gathering these files, walking to him, laying them at his feet and demanding, "Why?" Perhaps he would answer, perhaps he would shatter too; perhaps not. In some imagined future, they would sit at this very desk, coffee cooling, secrets confessed, a path opened between shadow and dawn. In this world, though, illusion is drowned beneath evidence. She is left with nothing but the bitter taste of what might have been.

The city calls below: horns, a siren wailing, the ceaseless promise and threat of New York at night.

Hana buries her face in her hands, shoulders wracked with silent sobs. The files spill onto the velvet, fanning across crimson and shadow. In the relentless hush, only one truth remains—love here was never safe, and the man she loved mapped every darkness with exquisite, unforgivable care.

Pages sprawl across Silas's mahogany desk and spill onto the floor, black and red ink circling names in Hana's restless hand. The city's glow has faded to an uncertain blue at the edges of the glass, dawn a thin ribbon pushing against the horizon. Her finger drags across signatures—Caius Drake, Lucien Blackwell, Darius Hale, Orion Vega—each a thread entwined through contracts, transfers, emails stamped with Brotherhood sigils. The air in the penthouse study tastes cold and metallic, tinged with the sharp ozone of static and a whiff of scorched printer paper. The carpet muffles her shifting knees. Every few breaths, she pauses to listen for footsteps beyond the silent door.

A name catches beneath her nail—Victor Kane, the specter she has heard only in wary whispers, now tethered by a spreadsheet to holdings Silas never spoke of. Selena Voss, her sharp font nested in a confidential memo—code words for "media leverage" and "quiet pressure" baring the shape of a woman who bends governments. Damian Locke, snakeskin watermarking a document that spells out blackmail and bones beneath polished boardrooms.

The files spill secrets that taste like copper on her tongue. Hana pulls another sheet close and circles the date of a wire transfer—millions sluiced from a charity auction to a shell company. Her pulse thrums, echoing the distant siren-call drifting from the street below. Another line leads to hospital settlements and the hush of medical error—Darius's world, mapped in litigation and cover-up. A footnote traces back to another rival: a tech start-up smothered before it drew breath, Orion's name a shadow behind the deletion.

She shuts her eyes and the study blurs out, bathed in the blue-grey tint of coming morning. Headlines bloom behind her eyelids: BROTHERHOOD SCANDAL EXPOSED. The city's gilded screens flicker one after another in her mind's eye. Silas's face, stoic and unreadable, at the center. The word 'philanthropist' will crack, replaced by 'liar' and 'criminal.' The Empire's glass façade will shatter—offices emptied, their lives rewritten, every act of quiet tenderness between these men and their families corrupted by the world's gaze. Caius's portfolio erased, Lucien's clients lost, Darius's medical license revoked, Orion's innovations discredited and folded into ashes.

She draws her knees to her chest on the velvet sofa, arms wrapped around the weight of printed paper. She can almost hear the conversations turning sour—the wives and partners glancing sideways, old wounds bared among friends. Police flashbulbs ignite behind her eyes, each revelation a detonation that splinters loyalty and trust. What becomes of the women who offered her warmth, sisterhood? What will become of her if she is seen as an accomplice or a traitor?

She pulls one crumpled page free and flattens it across her thigh, jaw tight, fingers trembling. Courage drags itself up, battered and uncertain, setting her heart against the dread pouring into her limbs.

Her voice carves the silence, raw as a wound.

"Why did you lie to me? Was I just another smudge to clean up?"

Light shifts on the ceiling, transforming Silas's study into a place she no longer recognizes. The city yawns awake beyond the glass, and she can't shake the ache of missing a future she had only started to dream.

She can hear the echo of Silas's words from the night before, soft and careful, threading promises through her hair. Now, every kindness feels suspect—motives shadowed, each touch reinterpreted as manipulation or damage control. She shoves the files aside and rubs her hands over her face.

Her mind tangles in argument, two voices echoing:

He did it all for them. For her.

He would never have let her see these things if any love was real at all.

If she walks away now, does she save herself or become the stone that topples his world? If she stays, can she ever stop doubting the look in his eyes, the grip of his hand on hers?

She stares out at the city, catching her own reflection—hollow-eyed, lost, no longer the girl who served lattes and guarded scars. The files twitch in her hands as sunrise finally touches the skyline, flecks of gold stuttering across towers and casting the air bone-pale.

Her internal debate builds until she can't bear the silence.

"Part of me wants to take this straight to him, demand to know every damned detail."

Her voice breaks, softer on the next breath.

"But if I do... if he tells me what I fear, what if there's nothing left to save?"

The room hums with emptiness. There are only two ends to this unraveling: confrontation or flight. Her thumb digs into the roughness of the last page. For a moment, she tries to summon her mother's voice from memory, some scrap of home, a reason to believe in new beginnings—then lets the ache anchor her instead.

The city's brightness bleeds into the study. Hana stands, bracing herself against the glass, the vast world at her feet. The pages are cold in her hands—every line, a fuse itching for flame. She breathes slowly, sets her jaw, and looks past the glass-and-steel horizon.

She readies herself to choose, to fight or abandon, as below, New York stirs in a thousand unknowing ways.

Shattered Trust

Midnight floods Silas's study with a hush, the world beyond its triple-glazed glass reduced to pulse and shadow—New York's lights flickering, distant and unreachable, across seams of steel and ink. Inside, the air holds the remnants of old paper and wood polish, heavy with secrets. Scattered across the mahogany table, printouts and files lie like forensic evidence: headlines, banking ledgers, encoded reports, the thin, clinical fonts bleeding under the warm cone of a desk lamp.

Hana stands amid the wreckage, her fingertips tracing the edge of a sheet that bears Victor Kane's name. The words blur, the weight of knowledge settling somewhere behind her ribcage—cold and raw, impossible to ignore. Her pulse thrums in her wrist, each beat betraying her calm as she waits. Then, the door opens with the soft click of authority, and Silas enters.

He pauses, closing the door quietly behind him, shoulders up and jaw fixed. A chill follows him—a contrast to the dust-muffled heat of the study. He moves carefully, as if aware of how every sound travels in this citadel of secrets. Silas's gaze lands first on the files, then on Hana.

Shadows carve sharp lines across his cheekbones, silver at his temples gleaming dully in the lamplight.

"Stay. Please." His voice is low, barely disturbing the hush. "Before you decide to go, just... hear me out." He comes closer, deliberate, a man measuring the distance between friend and foe.

Hana's eyes hold his, unblinking. In the silence, a siren wails somewhere far below, too faint to shatter the tension suspended here. She doesn't move, arms folded across her chest. Betrayal lodges in her throat, bitter and metallic.

Silas's hand comes to rest on the edge of the table, palm flat. "Everything you've found here—" His fingers curl around the mahogany, knuckles whitening. "The blackmail. The destroyed careers. Every manipulation with the press. It wasn't just for me. Or for power. I did it to shield the Brotherhood. To keep them safe... to keep you safe, once you stepped into this world."

He breathes in, shoulders rolling as if he's carrying the weight of each confession. For the first time, his words tremble, as if the truth itself could cut. "Those scandals, the smear campaigns—Victor Kane, Selena Voss, Damian Locke—they don't play by the rules. I had to outmaneuver them. If I'd hesitated, the Brotherhood would've burned. That's how far they'd go."

The room seems to shrink. Hana flicks her gaze between the files and Silas—searching for a crack, a trace of the man who'd once smiled at her across a café booth. All she finds is a mask of hunger and regret, twin fires burning in his eyes. She wonders if he's only ever shown her reflections—layers of strategy draped over bone and blood—if the man she wanted truly existed outside this latticework of sacrifice.

A thousand tangled thoughts churn inside her. How many times had she reached for his hand, seeking warmth, and how many times had that hand been orchestrating betrayals behind her back? Did he love her—or simply protect her as another asset caught in the wake of a war she never chose?

Would it be braver to believe him, or to turn away?

She imagines a future splintered by scandal: Kane's puppet masters ripping the Brotherhood's empire apart, headlines bearing Silas's name like a brand, her own face pixelated, standing on a curb, unmoored. Or another future—one where she stays. Accepts his darkness. Lets the shattered pieces fit together, even if the edges cut. Trusting, forgiving, risking it all for something more fragile than loyalty. But can she? What does it cost to abandon the last, precious part of herself that can say "no" to power?

The silence between them is ragged, suffocating. Silas draws a breath and tries again—his voice rough, words sheared down by hope and fear. "I never wanted you hurt. I never wanted this... for either of us. Every choice I made was about them, Hana. About all of us—about you, about a future where we could be safe. Sometimes I think I've lost myself in it. But I swear to you, it's not just about control—not when it comes to you. If there's a way to fix this... I'll do anything."

His shoulders sag. The danger is not just in the room but in every word unspoken, every secret that's calcified beneath the city lights outside. It hangs there, waiting for her to decide if she can unmake it.

A dialogue block cuts through the tension, brisk and ragged:

"Why didn't you tell me, Silas?" Her words taste like broken glass. "You said you trusted me. How can I believe a single thing after this?"

Silas's answer comes sanded and raw, his mouth tightening against the truth. "Because if I did, I'd put you in their crosshairs. Kane, Voss, Locke—they're not men and women, Hana, they're monsters. I'm sorry. I should've tried... but I was afraid the truth would tear us apart anyway."

A second dialogue block, her voice almost breaking now: "So you chose for me."

"I chose wrong, Hana. I know that," he whispers, misery burrowing deep across his features. "But I can't change what's done. I just—don't walk away. Not yet."

She doesn't respond. For several seconds, the study exists in a world with no clocks, no easy comfort. New York's heartbeat seeps faintly through glass and silk drapes. Each breath is heavier than the last, every shadow between them a question with no answer.

Hana's back is rigid, lips pressed into a tremor as she stands across the mahogany table from Silas. Shadows carve his features into granite—unknowable, distant. Around them, the study breathes in the hush of midnight, lamplight turned low, each paper strewn across the desk an accusation. Her hand, balled tight at her side, won't stop shaking. She lifts her chin slowly, her voice quiet but edged sharp as broken glass.

"I can't do this anymore, Silas." The words scrape her raw. "Every secret, every lie—maybe you told yourself it was protection, but you locked me out. You broke everything I ever believed about you. About us." Her eyes shine in the gloom, defiant and wounded. "All this time, I thought you were the man who saw me. But you were just hiding—behind power, behind control. How are these pieces supposed to fit together?"

Silas doesn't flinch. His face is set, but the pulse at his throat betrays him, fluttering fast. He watches her with a desperate, silent plea, but makes no move toward her. The air between them is charged, humming with pain, and Hana feels the weight of every concealed truth arrange itself on her shoulders. Something in her steadies; she straightens, feeling the old splinters of fear crack and fall away, replaced by a chilling sort of clarity. She steps back from the table, fingers brushing the cold edge for balance—like touching the truth one more time before letting it go.

"I can't stay here." Her voice trembles, but she bites it down, makes it strong. "Not in this room, in this world—twisted up with shadows and half-truths. I spent too long letting someone else decide who I could be." She draws a breath, the air thick with the library's musk and the faint, ghostly sweetness of dying roses. "This—" she gestures, taking in the files, the secrets, the fortress of Silas's making "—this is not healing. I need to find myself out there again. Away from your walls, away from a life where love is just another thing to be weaponized."

He moves suddenly—a desperate, involuntary surge—closing the space between them. His hand finds her wrist, not tight, but inescapable, pulse quick against her skin. His palm is warm, but the tension in his grip is unmistakable; it's a plea and a panic both. Hana stares down at his fingers, at the contradiction of gentleness and restraint, and feels the gulf between them widen even as his touch lingers.

"Hana, don't," Silas says, his voice fraying, rough at the edges. "I—If you go…"

She looks at him, the man who spun gold from shadows, who guarded the Brotherhood from monsters like Victor Kane and Selena Voss—rival empires and political predators, all circling for scraps. She sees the strategist behind every media scandal, the lover who held her quietly when she thought she'd splinter apart, and the stranger she's never quite known. There was a time she would have bent, would have let hope convince her to stay. Not now.

She gently twists her wrist free. The motion is soft, final.

"Let me go," she murmurs. "You can make the world bend for you, Silas. But you can't bend me."

There's a beat—a silence strung taut between them, thick with all the words unsaid. She crosses the study slowly, each step muffled by the rich Persian rug, pausing just long enough at the door to let her hand brush the cold brass. She glances back; Silas stands illuminated by the dim blue wash of city lights leaking through glass, hollowed and unmoving.

Her heart hammers against her ribs, but there's something fragile—almost sacred—in the aching certainty of her exit. She needs to reclaim it, whatever future waits outside these locked rooms.

For a breathless instant, silence pulses through the study. The solitude is tangible: the walls swallowing her scent, the city's distant, muffled noise pressing in from high above Manhattan. Hana's hand grips the handle, steady now, and she steps across the threshold, leaving the stale air of secrets behind.

The door snicks shut—a soft, definitive sound. It ricochets in the dimness, echoes curling into the hush like the last word in a doomed conversation. Silas is left staring at the empty patch of carpet where she once stood, at the stillness broken only by the faint hum of machines, the lost promise of a future that's already slipping into memory.

In their wake, the balance of power shifts. Trust is gone, stripped bare by exposure; love, a wounded thing retreating into shadow. Each stands changed by the rupture—Hana with her earned independence, Silas with the cold emptiness of loss—while outside, somewhere deep in the web of power and rivalry, enemies like Victor Kane and Selena Voss circle hungrily, ready to feed on every fracture left behind.

Silas stands rigid, staring at the closed door. Shadows cluster at his feet, thrown long by the dim amber glow of a desk lamp against the mahogany and charcoal of his private study. His fists are white-knuckled, pressed so tightly his knuckles ache, and when the silence finally settles—heavy, oppressive—he lets out a breath that quivers. His voice is barely a crack in the hush, almost unseen. "I've lost the only thing I never meant to risk."

Outside the triple-glazed windows, the city blazes—trains of light meander through the black lattice of Manhattan night, skyscrapers puncture clouds, and somewhere, sirens howl. The room swallows each sound, thick velvet absorbing the spikes of living that carry on so close, yet impossibly far. Silence thickens, almost living, crawling across the muted rug, seeping into the marrow of this space.

Memory slices him open: Hana's laughter skittering along these same bookshelves, scattering dust motes and tension, her feet bare against stone, her hair tumbling forward as she argued a point with the sharp grace of someone who refuses to flinch. He'd watch her fingers spin a stray orchid petal—always worrying at the details, always pulling at secrets until she found the vulnerable places even he forgot he owned. She'd look up and, for a fractured second, let him believe he was more than the sum of his armor.

He turns, almost expecting to find her there again, teasing smile in place, ready to cut through his brooding with one irreverent comment. But all that remains is the faint imprint of her palm on a cup—creamy ceramic, ringed with cooling coffee—perched at the edge of the desk. Her scarf, left behind in haste, still carries a whisper of her perfume: wild roses and something deeper, the ghost of petrichor after rain. The scent lingers, both balm and knife.

A chair sits slightly askew where she once perched, defiant, drawing battle lines with nothing but her gaze. Pages are strewn across the table—Brotherhood files, rings pressed in to mark where she'd gripped them, questions burning into the paper like acid. Each trace of her is a reminder: he invited ruin into the sanctuary of his secrets, and now ruin is all that holds him. The silence presses tighter. It is not peace, but the sound of something vast and essential breaking.

His mind claws backward, desperate for escape. He sees Hana in snatches—a flash of her hand in his, the heat in her eyes when she challenged him, the bittersweetness of their first kiss, salted with tears and hope. He tastes the memory of her laughter, the feel of her breath ghosting along his jaw. Yet all of it feels impossibly distant, like echoes warped by time and grief. Each memory is a wound, fresh and bleeding, that control cannot cauterize.

He stalks to the window and braces both hands against cold glass. The city sprawls beneath him; a living, humming thing. Down there, rival media icons like Victor Kane are orchestrating campaigns that gnaw at Silas's empire, spreading venom in headlines and whispers. Selena Voss, queen of political shadows, unspools scandals with ruthless precision—her phoenix tattoo a mocking sigil for rebirth born of other people's ashes. Damian Locke pushes corporate raiders into his flanks, biting at the vulnerable places exposed by recent fractures.

Even the Brotherhood itself is a house built on shifting fault lines. Loyalties fray as brothers look sideways, weighing the cost of keeping secrets against the threat of exposure. Tension sours once-unshakable bonds: Caius's measured coldness, Lucien's wary silences, Orion's restlessness. And now—the deepest secret, the scandal he buried beneath layers of denial, is close enough to the surface that Silas can feel it pulse at his throat, waiting to detonate and tear everything apart. His private heartbreak is a fissure running through the strongest foundation he's ever known, inviting every enemy to exploit the open wound.

Guilt gnaws through him. Every sacrifice he made to keep Hana and the Brotherhood safe, every lie spun on the altar of protection, now feels like rot spreading from the inside out. He questions—again, and again—whether love was foolish for a man forged in secrecy, or whether believing in the possibility of more was the real betrayal. Chilled by the air, Silas wonders if he is condemned to solitude by his own making—a king haunted by ghosts in a glass fortress, cut off from the only warmth he's ever wanted.

He forces his spine straighter, turning grief into the steel of resolve. The city below is alive with threat, yes, but it's alive with opportunity too. There is no room for softness now: not with Victor's venom, Selena's sabotage, Damian's shadow army closing in. Not with the Brotherhood's unity splintering. He must patch the fragile alliances, close ranks, and step into the tempest of knives. If there remains any path forward—toward Hana, toward redemption—it lies in fighting for what he nearly let slip away.

The hum of distant traffic claws at the glass. Silas inhales, scenting only paper, old roses—ashes and the faint promise of something growing. He turns from the window. In the suffocating hush of his study, every second etches the border between what is lost and what might be saved.

Fractured Hearts

A single lamp casts a weak golden pool over the mess of books and rumpled throws in Hana's apartment. She sits cross-legged on her battered blue couch, knees drawn up, the faded upholstery prickling the bare skin behind her calves. The air carries traces of old espresso and last night's rain, half-stale and thick with her own warmth. Outside, the city offers only distant engine groans and a hush broken now and then by someone's laughter—always muffled by her double-paned windows, always faint, as if the world has moved on without her.

In her hands, a photograph: herself, months ago, before the storm. Her hair is brighter, cheeks round with hope, her smile open—oblivious to what would come after. She stares at that girl, searching for recognition with stinging eyes. Her thumb wanders the glossy surface, tracing the upturned curve of the mouth, needing to feel something solid, even if it's only a ghost. A tear drops, smearing a watery line across the memory, blurring the boundary between then and now.

She brings the photo closer until her breath fogs it, heat from her lips warping the surface.

Her body folds inward, spine pressed to the cool concrete wall, the world outside reduced to shadow and vibration. Clutching the photo to her chest, she shuts her eyes and lets old moments reel by: Silas's rare laughter fizzing through bitter black coffee, the careful brush of his jacket over her shoulders in a February wind, the fleeting warmth of his hand catching her wrist when she almost walked away for good. The memory of his smile—never quite reckless, never quite safe—shakes loose a thousand splinters beneath her skin. She had answered that smile with one of her own once, softening, trusting.

She lets herself remember the other side, too. The moments she dared to lean into his world, cracked her shell to let him see something real: late nights full of stories, secrets exchanged in hushes, her fingers tangling with his over rose thorns. Every time she let down her guard, hope bloomed—even when it scraped raw. She remembers too well the price of such hope: the way his eyes would grow steely right after they softened, how words came with edges sharper than any gift he gave. She had learned the hard way that in the world Silas navigated, admission meant ammunition, and a chink in your armor could bury you.

Her chest aches. She whispers to the empty room, her voice dry as parchment, "Maybe I was only ever fooling myself." The words break apart soft as dust, hanging above the cluttered table and stacks of unopened mail. Maybe she's always been good at this—seeing what she wants in someone's eyes, ignoring everything sharper. Maybe the fantasy of being loved survives longer than love itself.

Her apartment presses in. Laundry towers where she abandoned it; a half-empty mug winks from the windowsill. She breathes, sharp and shallow. The scents in the room reek of her failures: burnt toast, cheap shampoo, the metallic tang of coins scraped together for next month's rent. She remembers, suddenly, the first time debt threatened to swallow her whole, before Silas, before the Brotherhood—a younger Hana, hungry and cornered, swearing never to need anyone. She thinks of every promise she's made to herself and wonders which one she broke first.

Her grip tightens on the photo. She wants to believe there's a way back to the girl in the picture—a version of herself unsullied by secrecy and loss. Still, the city's darkness claws at the window; the world beyond is full of men like Silas, sharks circling in tailored suits. Victor Kane, the media wolf who hounded the Brotherhood's every misstep; Selena Voss with her eyes of glacial calculation and her taste for ruin. Damian Locke waits in the wings, ready to devour the weak. In their world, vulnerability is a currency spent only once, trust a line drawn in vanishing ink.

A soft chime breaks her reverie. Her phone lights up, the screen bleaching her face with its cold glow. The string of unread messages stretches across the glass—his name at the top, then another from Lucien, two from Seraphine, and a host of others. The Brotherhood's concern is a web—its strands tightening around her even here, even now. She holds the device, her thumb hovering. A beat passes.

Then, with a snap decision, she presses her thumb until the screen dies and tosses the phone where it can't tempt her—down into the empty laundry basket, deep beneath a heap of unwashed clothes. Silence reclaims the space.

Muscles trembling, Hana draws her legs beneath her, arms wrapping tight around her knees. She burrows into herself, shutting out both the pale lamplight and the ceaseless city glare. In the half-dark, she is a knot of breath and memory—shivering on a couch that holds the shape of a loneliness she never meant to invite but can't manage to drive out.

Silas Carver moves through the shadows of his penthouse office like a ghost searching for faults in the fortress he's built—soundless but for the soft, metronomic click of Italian leather shoes over polished marble. The night hums beyond glass walls, the spill of city lights smearing the black windows in soft golds and hard blues. His suit jacket slouches on one shoulder; he wears the armor, but the lines beneath betray sleeplessness. Each call from Shanghai, Dubai, Zürich is fielded with the voice of a man whose patience is measured in milliseconds. He answers with clipped words, his tone cold enough to freeze negotiations if not for the weight behind his name.

"Add twelve points to the counteroffensive. I don't care if Kane's lawyers threaten sanctions—pull the feeds if they escalate. No distractions."

Silas drags a hand over his jaw, feeling the hint of stubble, the familiar irritation of a face that's been unwatched for too long. Across the world, Victor Kane's influence festers in gossip and coded threats, the hostile voice of a rival who wants the Brotherhood razed and Carver's empire gutted clean. Other enemies—Selena Voss, ice-veined and relentless from her political throne, and Damian Locke, sending up smoke signals from Chicago's hungry underbelly—tighten the net. Silas barks orders, moods flickering with the sharp light of too many screens. None meet the eyes staring back from the dark reflection behind him.

When the last call sputters out, he faces the digital map spanning the far wall. Encrypted symbols bloom with fresh warnings: anonymous tips, hostile asset movement, legal shadows flickering near the edges of their holdings. Zoom in—London, Paris, D.C.—the Brotherhood's reach feels suddenly thin. Silas's gaze rakes each data point, and the muscles in his neck knot, evidence of an empire under siege. Static from security reports crackles; it tastes of ozone, metal, a storm pressing hard on his veins.

A single hum pulses beneath all the noise—the office always feeds him music, a low cello shiver, but tonight the notes seem to mourn instead of fortify. He slides a finger over a control, silencing it. Absence swells, tighter than the knot in his chest.

His hands hover above his desk as if wary to touch its emptiness. All except the rose, left alone in a sea of black glass. One long-stemmed bloom, petals deep as blood, edges curling just so—a flower Hana pressed into his palm that storm-soaked night months before. He picks it up; the stem prickles beneath his thumb, but he refuses to flinch. Holding the rose, Silas breathes slowly, tongue pressed to his teeth as if taste could conjure the memory of her perfume, the hint of oranges and winter wind that always clung to her skin.

He remembers her laughter, quick and bright as summer thunder, how she stared at him with open defiance, as though she saw through every mask he'd learned to wear. He remembers, too, the last time she closed his door behind her—no arguments, just the hush that follows things breaking.

The rose quivers in his hand.

"She never wanted this," he rasps, his voice gone raw. "None of them ever do."

He knows work is his way through the pain; blind focus, the rote act of control. This was the lesson his father taught: never let softness eat you alive. The memory of his mother—her bruised velvet voice, her hand brushing the hair from his eyes before she vanished into the past—clings to him as much as the legacy he inherited, a legacy where vulnerability equates to annihilation. Protect the Brotherhood. Win the war. Smother what threatens to undo you.

But the calculations blur now. Hana's face haunts the periphery, every tender word unspoken curdling into regret. His instincts scream for order, for a strategy that wipes her ghost from the walls, that repels the circling predators—the Kanes, the Selena Vosses, the Lockes with their serpentine ambition.

He sets the rose down too abruptly. Petals bruise, and the scent lifts—dusky, bitter.

At his console, he types furiously, knuckles pale as bone. Reports flood the screen—cyberattacks spidering down European satellites, lawsuits crackling like distant thunder, rumors spat from shadowy sources. Every urgent missive a battlefield, every keystroke meant to fill the void she's left. But control takes more effort now; focus fractures around the edges.

His vision dances between numbers and shadows. There's Hana in the glint of the glass. There's his past in the trembling rose. Neither will let him go. How easy, once, to cloak himself in detachment. How hard now not to shatter under the weight of so much missing.

When the last window finally closes, Silas rises. Fingers flick the light switch, plunging the office into near darkness—and all at once, the city is there, cold but ablaze, a universe of stories spinning beyond his own relentless orbit. His reflection hovers in the window, all hard lines, eyes ringed with the ache of wanting—something he can neither command nor calculate.

He doesn't move, anchored by regret and the press of coming trouble, the silent war outside now mirrored inside. Alone, Silas Carver stands rigid before the empty city, and the sorrow in the room almost tastes real.

Rainwater slides in blurred ribbons down the bombproof glass set high above the basement depths, each drop distorting the thin shaft of orange streetlight that penetrates the gloom of the Brotherhood's secret clubhouse beneath an unmarked Manhattan street. The air carries a lingering whiff of burned coffee and polished wood, the kind of undertone that seeps into skin after too many nights laying out war. Caius Drake enters first, mechanical in his efficiency, shrugging out of his coat as the security lock hisses shut behind him. His footsteps echo—one-two—against ancient brick and rich, lacquered mahogany, always the first to face danger head-on, even as exhaustion shadows his brow.

Lucien Blackwell waits at the far end of the oval table, suit immaculate, hands interlocked as though physically restraining turmoil. Darius hovers nearby, muscles tense beneath his surgical scrubs, the blue fabric stained at one sleeve from a hasty detour from the hospital. Orion slouches by the wall, tapping out a restless code on his tablet, illuminated by a silver glow fracturing his face in sharp angles. The only other light is the pendulum glare of bulbs overhead, flickering slightly—a reminder that nothing in this bunker lasts forever.

Caius drops a file onto the table with a muted thud.

"We're being hit from three sides. Somebody's paying Vanderson Labs to dig up old ghosts—contracts, stock manipulation, you know the drill. They're more aggressive than they've been in years," he says, his voice low and jaw tight. His hand curves into a fist atop the wood, veins stark in sharp relief. "This isn't lashing out for leverage. This feels personal."

Lucien exhales, leaning back so his chair creaks. "Two media outlets published exposés this morning. They kept quiet about their sources, but the dots line up—litigation I buried last year, suddenly unearthed. Names we all know. There's a judge—Fellman—who's supposed to be out. I had him handled." Lucien massages his brow, frustration edged by a legal mind that seldom allows chaos. "He's not out. Someone's reanimating corpses and pointing them at us."

"I know those names," Darius says. He runs a hand through his hair, sweat sheening his temple despite the club's unyielding chill. "I treated Vanderson's fixer once—broken ribs, back in June. He said too much under anesthesia. There's chatter about sabotage—hacks, bribes, blackmail. Our security's thin, with Silas...not here."

"Silas would have sorted them in two phone calls," Orion mutters, stylus rapping harder on the tablet. His eyes dart along code, jaw clenched. "We lost three internal firewalls last night. Got two attempts on the core routers since dawn. I can handle the backend, but every move we make draws another spider. This is a coordinated attack—maybe Kane, maybe Vanderson, maybe both working under the table with God knows who. I need Silas's eyes. I'm not a phantom like him."

The men lapse into silence, the hum of servers and the city beneath their feet the only sound. Caius watches tension ripple between them, the way Darius's hand lingers by his phone, Lucien's knuckles whiten above legal pads, Orion's shoulders knot with kinetic nerves. The Brotherhood has always leaned on Silas, the strategist, the dead-eyed conductor who saw forward five moves and stitched their chaos into order. Without him, the cracks widen.

Trust was always their unspoken currency; now, suspicion creeps in by inches. Vanderson Labs is fuel on old wounds, reigniting memories of double-crosses, courtroom betrayals, and the day the Brotherhood nearly shattered when one of their own was set up and bled dry. Caius's own scars itch with memory, rage, and something worse—fear that this time, the opposition is cleverer, more patient, better resourced. Victor Kane, the unblinking vulture, and Selena Voss, the shadowed queen in the halls of power, orchestrate this storm. Caius smells the same rot: rumors planted in financial markets, legal tripwires, digital knives aimed at their backs. The room tastes of old blood and new panic.

He wants to snap—tell them to pull themselves together, to stop acting like orphans. He swallows the urge, knowing that holding the Brotherhood together is no longer just Silas's burden. If Silas refuses to stand at the center, someone has to—or each man will tear at the legacy until nothing remains but fractured empires and the ghosts of trust.

Lucien shifts first, his voice drier than before. "What's the plan, Caius? Waiting for our strategist to have an epiphany?"

"Or you could admit we're hemorrhaging and do something drastic for once," Orion fires back, too loud in the stifling dark. "I'm not the only one who's noticed, right? We can't outwait our enemies if half our people are hiding."

Darius's voice is quieter. "We can't replace Silas. That doesn't mean we do nothing. If we break apart now, we lose more than money."

Caius closes his hand around the edge of the table. "We adapt, or we lose. Falling apart is not an option—not with Kane and Voss hunting us. We cover each other's blind spots until Silas wakes up, or we find a new center. Don't look to me for miracles—do your damn jobs."

Tension coils in the walls. For a moment, the men's eyes meet—a flicker of solidarity, but also something fragile, half-broken. The silence settles again, heavier, as threats prowl unseen in the city above and the Brotherhood waits, leaderless, on the verge of unraveling.

The city outside Hana's window is draped in bruised indigo, street-lights dripping golden veins across rain-wet pavement far below. The faint hum of distant engines and the shudder of a subway moving underground are the only intrusions into the hush that has settled over her apartment. She sits cross-legged on the scarred floorboards, back pressed to chilled glass, the pocket warmth of her phone in her hand. Light from a single lamp carves soft halos through dust motes drifting above the ancient books and scattered receipts cluttering her living room.

Seraphine's message glows on the cracked screen, the words gentle and insistent as a lullaby. "Strength doesn't mean facing darkness alone. You still have family here, Hana." The text is short—deliberate. Not pity, but presence. Hana reads it again, letting each syllable settle. There is a tautness in her throat she does not trust; the kind of ache she thought she'd left behind when she learned to dodge questions and walk away before anyone could disappoint her.

Tears well without warning, and she blinks hard, impatient. She can taste the salt at the corners of her lips. Outside, a horn blares, long and distant, and her breath hitches, her body trembling in sudden answer. Seraphine's kindness cuts more deeply than any insult could—there is no armor against gentleness, especially when the world expects you to pick up your own shattered pieces.

Across the room, a vase on the chipped table holds what's left of Silas's latest overture—black and crimson petals curling at their edges, a scent of wilting regret lingering with the memory of his voice. Hana finds herself staring at them, measuring the distance between what was and what might have been. The roses are beautiful, even as they surrender—still striking, magnetic, but doomed to decay. She knows the message hidden in their gloom: beauty born of ashes, but only for those who survive the fire.

She presses her thumb to the screen, reading Seraphine's words until her vision blurs. In this dim, quiet haven, she allows herself to imagine. What if she had chosen to let Silas shoulder her burdens, allowed herself to believe that love could ever be sanctuary? Would that have saved her, or merely rewritten the flavor of her brokenness? She can see herself—just for a moment—leaning against his chest in a world where they face the storm as a unit. Sometimes, that vision is a bright possibility. Other times, it feels like stepping onto thin ice, every heartbeat a warning.

Hana's thoughts spiral outward. Could she be strong enough to accept help and not be devoured by debt—emotional, financial, or otherwise? Healing is not gentle. It is jagged and slow and costs more than she sometimes feels she has to give. What if the price of hope is washing herself raw in vulnerability that, if betrayed, may never heal? Can she risk the little self-worth she's gathered to a storm that might wash it away again, as swiftly as Victor Kane or Selena Voss would siphon away a fortune? There is the fear that in trying to stand unbroken beside Silas, she will lose even herself.

A creak from the radiator draws her back. She smooths the screen, folds her knees tighter to her body. She thinks of Seraphine, of Elara, of Amara—a circle built not of blood, but of surviving bruises together. Friendship, she's realizing, is not a chain that traps, but a line thrown to a drowning sailor. It's fragile, yes, but sometimes it's everything.

Lucien leans forward, forearms bracing the table edge, a deliberate distance closing between him and Silas. The room is soundproofed, the city's distant pulse snuffed to a breathless hush. Light glints off the silver scar at Silas's jaw as he stares at the note in his hand, Hana's handwriting tight, uncertain. Silas's voice is cracked and hushed, roughened by hours of rehearsed indifference torn thin.

"I don't want to lose her." His fingers dig into the tabletop as though anchoring himself. "If I do—if I lose her, the Brotherhood will follow. There's too much riding on us. My mistakes…I can't shield them from this fallout. Not anymore."

"None of us asked you to carry it all," Lucien says, measured, the lawyer's mask gentling a fraction. "She made you hope. But you made us believe the Brotherhood was unbreakable. Maybe it's time that isn't just on you."

"It was always meant to be on me," Silas whispers, letting the paper drop. "My father, my mother—loss is all I know. But I chose Hana. And I won't let her be collateral."

Hana wipes her cheeks, her voice trembling but resolute. "I have to survive this," she says—speaking to the silent room, to invisible ghosts, to herself. Shadows pool against her bare feet, but she sits upright, chin tipped toward the cold glow of Greenwich Village. Her grief is not silent submission any longer. It's the quiver before rising.

Silas exhales, his throat rasping with something dangerously close to hope. "Whatever comes, I can't run anymore."

So separated by glass, by city blocks, by the web of threats Victor Kane and Selena Voss have already begun to spin in the darkness, Hana and Silas sit, the relics of love and loss held between them—the roses drooping in one world, a note smoothed flat in another. Night presses in, uncertain, but neither yields. Not now. Not yet.

The Brotherhood Threatened

Caius stands stiffly by his window. Night covers the tall buildings on Wall Street in a dark blue shade. Below, the city moves quietly behind glass and tall towers. He holds a heavy paper report—too important to send digitally. The window feels cold, and his reflection looks as sharp as the city skyline. His advisor stands close, speaking quickly as if he is dealing with a big problem.

"They're joining forces—Vargo and the Petrova Group. They're betting against your index funds, sir. Rumors are already spreading in London—people say you might go broke." The advisor's voice shakes despite his attempt to sound calm.

Caius tightens his jaw, watching colorful lights move on a tall building. "No leaks. Tighten security. No emails out. No press releases. Use emergency rules. If anyone even talks to outsiders, fire them." The air in the office is tense, smelling of sweat and strong cologne.

In Midtown, Lucien sits calmly in his modern law office. The glass walls reveal everything inside, pretending to be open while hiding secrets. Paralegals move quickly, looking tired. Lucien opens a pale blue envelope marked PRIVATE. His heart races.

A senior lawyer enters quickly, holding a tablet. "Ava Kane, that reporter from Kane Media, has filed legal papers in federal court. She's investigating the Oakes case—your sealed record—and linking it to us." The room grows silent. Lucien grips the papers tightly. Sweat forms on his neck.

In the hospital, Darius walks faster down the hallway. Beeping machines and the antiseptic smell mix with worry. Lila waits at the front desk, holding her phone nervously.

She shows him the screen—emails with his name and headlines that cut like knives: 'Hale-Moreno Accused: Careless or Harmful?' Darius feels his throat tighten. Nurses whisper nearby, their backs straightening. The administrator calls sharply, "Dr. Hale, Ms. Moreno, boardroom now. Emergency meeting. Bring all papers."

Lila's hand shakes as she touches his. He squeezes her fingers gently, trying to stay calm, but inside he feels fear.

High above in his media center, Silas watches many screens. The headlines flash: 'Orion Club: Crimes Reported.' 'Carver Linked to Secret Money?' Comments flood in—threats and messages from fake accounts. His hands tighten as he scrolls. The attacks are harsh and planned. He thought he controlled the news, but now enemies are copying him.

Far away, Victor Kane works from a London penthouse, pushing plans across time zones. Selena Voss, a dangerous woman in power, makes deals in Washington D.C. Damian Locke moves money quietly through complex investments. Silas knows their methods—each attack is planned and cruel, based on old grudges that only get worse.

The city, with its steel and glass, is built for battles where powerful people trade secrets, and money talks louder than truth. Finance, law, medicine, media—they all link like a circle eating its own tail. Wars start and end in secret, always with old enemies and new rules.

Fear crawls under Silas's skin. The weight of responsibility is heavier than the empire he built. This is not just about bad news, money, or gossip—it is a direct attack on their foundation. The worst part is that he might lose control, and his silence could be used against him.

He thinks of Hana—her laugh, her tired smile when she thinks he isn't watching. Of his brothers, each alone, holding on to their legacy as their worlds fall apart. His mind plans each move, cold logic clashing with the idea that maybe this time, their world will break.

"I want updates every ten minutes. Cut all communication lines," Caius orders, his voice sharp.

"The staff are scared. Do we respond or stay quiet?" Lucien asks quietly.

"We stay calm. We show strength. No fuel for rumors," Darius says, but his grip on Lila's hand shows his worry.

Silas's finger rests on the silent alarm—no sirens here, just a soft light flashing. Four men, four places, all under attack. They hold proof that the world is shifting. The silent alarm calls them to unite. The city watches, waiting for them to fall.

Without a word, the fight begins.

Below the city, the Brotherhood's meeting room glows with a cold blue light. Caius stands at the head of the table, his suit tight and his eyes sharp in the dark. Silas watches the slight twitch in Caius's jaw—a sign he only shows here.

Caius raises one finger silently, and the security guards leave like shadows. Screens show stock numbers falling rapidly. Tomas Vargo's name glows red.

"Tomas started it," Caius says calmly, though his hands are white from gripping the table. "He planned the attacks—hostile takeovers, betting against stocks, false rumors about us going broke. Vargo's fingerprints are on every panic call."

Silence fills the room. Seraphina sits nearby, tense, meeting Caius's look with quiet dread.

Lucien pulls up encrypted files on a tablet, legal documents flashing across the screen. His face is tight, hiding fear. Next to him, Mariel watches carefully.

"Ava Kane filed subpoenas," Lucien says firmly. "She's digging into the closed case. Witnesses are talking. If this goes public, not just I, but the whole Brotherhood will be in trouble."

Screens change. Names and documents blur. Fear grows like sweat under collars.

Darius waits, shoulders hunched, still in scrubs. Lila holds his arm, shaking, hiding her face. Darius glances at her, almost unnoticed except by Silas.

"The board, led by Dr. Harper, wants independent checks. They may suspend our licenses. Ours," he says, looking at Lila and Orion. Orion taps his fingers nervously beside Elara's data sheets.

Whispers spread between disbelief and defense. Lila straightens, blinking away tears. Seraphina slides her a glass of water—silent support.

Orion breaks the tense silence, energy flashing. He shows the live social media dashboard—negative trends spike, online attacks flood their charity's name.

"Damian Kade's bots are attacking all our fronts. If we lose control of the story, we're finished before the market opens."

Elara swipes her screen, data flowing in. "This attack isn't random. Someone feeds it every hour. Vargo, Kade, Ava—they're working together, maybe more. And the support comes from beyond our country." She looks at Orion, sharing the heavy truth silently.

Silas sees stress everywhere. Caius's jaw is tense enough to break bones. Darius squeezes Lila's hand. Lucien scratches his tie—a habit when nervous. Seraphina, Amara, Mariel, and Elara talk quickly—either to build trust or doubt. Hana, quiet beside Silas, presses her nails into her palms, watching him more than the screens.

Trust once held them together. Now it frays with old secrets—Lucien's past nearly ruined Caius, Orion's mistakes cost Darius money, Silas's silence risked betrayal. Silas feels their glances questioning him, trust turning to suspicion.

Caius whispers, "If we had all the facts, maybe we'd stand a chance."

Lucien answers sharply, "What use are facts when truth is a weapon?"

Darius sighs, "I wish we weren't fighting blind."

Orion stands, frustrated, "We built this to protect us, not to die."

Silas feels the weight of leadership. He prepares to speak but hesitates. Memories of past promises hang between them.

Tonight, some lines won't be crossed.

The crisis alert sounds. Silence falls. Everyone waits for Silas to speak, hope and fear tight inside. His secret grows, a shadow behind him.

No one breaks the silence.

Night presses against Silas Carver's penthouse windows. Manhattan glows far below, unaware. The lounge is dim, light shining on a crystal decanter and a bright red rug. Hana stands at the edge, arms crossed against the cold.

Silas gestures to a chair. "Sit, Hana." His voice is low and serious. She moves quietly, her slippers soft on the floor, his cologne mixing with the cold air. She looks older, with dark circles under her eyes, ready for a fight she didn't want.

He sets a folder on the table. Inside are names, numbers, and secret papers—proof of power built on hidden choices. "If this gets out," he says softly, "the Brotherhood falls. Everything I built, everyone I protect... gone. Including you. They'll blame you just for knowing."

Hana holds her breath but doesn't cry. Her knuckles turn white as she grips her knees. Her eyes look toward the dark window. "Why tell me now? Is this a warning or a confession?"

He looks away, city lights shining in his eyes. He carries this alone—a heavy burden from lessons, memories, and loss. Hana's strength and understanding have become his anchor and weakness.

The moment breaks as Caius and Lucien enter. The elevator chime announces them. Caius storms in, wet from the rain, his face set for battle. He slams a folder full of market chaos onto the table.

"No more secrets, Silas," Caius demands. "You want to lead? Tell us how deep this goes. Vargo's using your secrets, and my fund's under attack. How much is on you?"

Lucien stands at the door, watching closely. Quiet but fierce: "We can't fight blind, Silas. If you hide things, you make us all targets. We need everything to protect what's left."

The room grows tense. Hana stands, her voice trembling but strong. "He's right. We can't ask for trust while withholding secrets. Do you really think only you can bear this? What if that breaks us?"

She looks at Silas—not angry, but tired and hopeful. "We survive together, or we don't. We deserve all the truth, not just me."

Silas grips the armrest, breathing slowly. He is both boy and man, leader and lonely. If he shares all old wounds and secrets, they will be vulnerable. But maybe his walls will bring ruin.

He hears his father's warning: trusting is risky. But Hana's courage reminds him of his mother's faith—he must trust more than just armor.

He imagines the future—one where he shares all and risks losing the brotherhood, and another where he keeps silent and loses love.

He stands, calm yet firm. "I will act," he says. "But not everything can be shared now. I'll keep you all safe." The city lights outline him as he leads Hana away. She looks back, silently asking to be let in. Caius and Lucien exchange a look—understanding and warning.

The penthouse closes in, full of secrets. Outside, the city watches and waits.

The war room hums quietly, filled with tension. The Brotherhood meets, faces lit by blue screens showing numbers and enemy names. Caius stands by the main board, lists growing as stock prices fall. Tomas Vargo's name shines red, a warning.

Orion taps keys, drawing lines between data points on glowing screens. Darius sits back, tense, glancing at Lila's latest media report and Silas's hard face. Lucien's eyes flash sharp. He gives quick legal orders as the team works.

At the table's edge, Silas watches enemy profiles grow and shrink. News feeds flicker threats. Victor Kane's photo glares, a predator in a suit. Next to him, Selena Voss looks cold and daring. Damian Kade's file glows like a snake, with data showing his attacks.

Silas sees the patterns under the chaos—Victor's plans, media storms that almost destroyed them, Selena's quiet moves to ruin their secrets. Outside, Manhattan sleeps, but here, they know what will break if they fail.

Caius writes quickly: "Block brokers. Buy out Vargo's holdings. Use decoys. Cut their data lines." His voice is calm, but his jaw is tight. Darius whispers counterplans, haunted by past losses. Lila holds his arm, steadying him.

Lucien starts his legal fight. Subpoenas pop up on his tablet. "Get injunctions by morning. Martin's team hunts leaks. Trace Ava Kane's sources, stop her claims first." His tone is hard but tired—old wounds not healed.

Orion laughs dryly. "Our social media is crashing," he says, nodding to Elara, who scans hashtags like sifting through debris. "Damian's bots spread lies. If we don't block them soon, we're finished before dawn." She pulls up new defenses on her laptop.

Silas watches them gather strength but remembers when Victor first attacked their reputation—how it felt to face rumors and threats. Victor's words were smooth lies hiding sharp danger. Silas fought back hard then, breaking ties and wiping data to save the Brotherhood. He trusted no one, not even his closest.

Now, as Orion codes defenses and Lucien leads legal attacks, as Darius holds Lila's hand steady, Silas feels his old armor crack. He thinks of Hana, who never flinched when he showed her his secrets. She asked if control was worth the loneliness it brought. He tells himself yes—but wonders how many costs until nothing is left to save.

"They'll hit harder now," Lucien says quietly, watching files open.

Caius's voice is firm, "Let them try. They think we're broken—let's show them what we really are."

"We need allies outside this room," Orion adds. "Not just tech people. Real friends, influencers, ground support."

Lucien scoffs. "Since when do you trust anyone?"

Orion smiles, ready to fight. "I trust results. Always have."

Darius clears his throat, tension in his hands. "We are still standing. That's more than most could say."

Silas holds their words close as maps and threats change on the screens. Sweat forms on his forehead. He catches Caius's hand—steady and sure. Others join—Lucien, Darius, Orion, Lila's light touch on Darius. In the quiet of the night, their resolve grows.

When they stand, the city's glow is faint outside. But inside, where legacy, danger, and loyalty mix, they are strong. Dawn is not a promise—it's a test. The Brotherhood will face it.

Hana in the Crossfire

The city night wears its secrets like a shroud. Hana steps from her apartment, the door clicking shut with a shaky finality behind her. Keys bite into her palm, her fingers gone pale with strain. On this quiet Greenwich Village street, the hush feels unnatural—coiled, tense, as if the darkness itself lies in wait. Somewhere in the distance, a dog barks. The only light comes from the jaundiced lantern above her stoop, casting a bruised shadow across the sidewalk's broken seams.

Each step is a negotiation between caution and necessity. The rattle of her breath escapes in sharp bursts, silvering the air. She glances over her shoulder. No one—yet every instinct prickles. Her past taught her to trust what her eyes missed. Corners had teeth; shadows kept secrets.

A bulb flickers overhead as she turns onto the main street, painting the wet asphalt in stuttering gold. Manhattan always hums with life, but tonight the city pulses on a quieter frequency. A trash can overturns further up the block. Rooftop vents gasp stale warmth. Someone's laughter rides a gust from a hidden window, brittle and far away.

Then—footsteps.

Hana's body tightens. Sharp, measured. The slap of soles grows louder, hurried, hungry. When she reaches the edge of the sidewalk, her heart hammers out a frantic warning. She sucks in cold air stained with car exhaust and burned coffee grounds from the closed café across the street.

She ducks down a side alley—narrow, walls pressed close and slick with old rain. The world shrinks to the alley's throat. A rusted dumpster sits askew, the metal reeking of rot and bleach. Before her mind registers more, they appear—two figures, faces obscured beneath black balaclavas, shoulders bulked out by thick coats. Their presence is a wall, cutting off retreat.

The first man's voice is warped, as if passed through a broken radio. "You hold your tongue. Forget what you saw, what you know about Orion. You breathe a word—"

The second steps forward, gloved hand reaching. "Tell Carver we're watching. Silas can't keep you—can't keep any of them—safe."

It's not rage that bursts inside Hana at his words, not at first, but a raw and sticky fear. The kind she remembers from nights spent hiding from her ex, from debt collectors who spat her last name like a curse. But this is different. These men ooze power, confidence—a threat shaped by people like Victor Kane, Damian Locke, Selena Voss. Names she barely dares whisper but now bleed into her reality.

She lunges. The world narrows to the burning grip on her wrist, the stink of latex and cigarette smoke. She wrenches free, skin scraping the dumpster's corroded edge—a line of fire scoring her arm. Her feet slam on concrete. The alley warps into a tunnel of adrenaline and echoing terror. She hears one bark a curse behind her, heavy footfalls crashing after her as she emerges onto the main road, chest tight, lungs clawing for air.

The city accepts her—horns, headlights, the flood of a nearby bodega's cheap neon sign. Only now does the chase falter; she staggers, dizzy, into the glowing pool at the door. In the kaleidoscope of lamplight, her vision sifts through tremors. At her feet—a white envelope. Its paper is almost luminous, pristine amid litter and stubbed-out cigarettes. She picks it up, trembling as she cracks the seal.

Inside, a message in stark, mechanical block letters:

STAY QUIET OR NEXT TIME, IT'S BLOOD—TELL SILAS WE ARE WATCHING.

Her mouth tastes of copper, her heartbeat loud enough she half-expects the cashier inside to hear. The truths she'd denied for weeks twist into clarity: Silas might be a fortress, but that meant she was a window someone could break. They knew her name. They watched. This was Victor Kane's playbook—intimidate, isolate, then scorch the ground beneath your enemies.

She stumbles into the bodega, warmth brushing against her clammy cheeks, fluorescent lights too bright and cold. She fumbles past shelves of boxed noodles and dusty candy, pushing into the restroom at the back. The door shuts. Lock clicks. She backs up until porcelain meets her spine.

Her thoughts spiral, a cyclone of memory and fresh terror. Once, she ran from an ex-boyfriend who made threats for the thrill. She battled debt collectors, changed jobs, changed addresses. That taught her how to survive. But the fear now—its shape is new. Its claws are sharper. To be hunted not for weakness but for knowing too much; to realize Silas's world had bled into hers, and what she loved might destroy her.

Trembling, she calls Silas.

"They—" Her voice is rough, every word scraped raw. "Two men in masks. In the alley by my apartment. They knew me. Said to tell you… they're watching. Gave me a note. Said blood would come next."

"You're safe now? Where are you?" His tone is steel caressed by panic.

"I ran into the bodega on Eighth. I'm locked in the bathroom. Silas, I—" Her voice cracks on a breath. "I'm done being scared. But I'm angry too. Do you understand? I can't—won't—live like I'm prey."

"I'll handle this. No one will touch you. Lock the door. Wait for my people." He's all command—cold, certain, never showing the fear she feels humming through the line.

"Silas, promise—"

"I promise."

She presses her forehead to the frigid tile wall. The world smells of bleach and old sweat, her own skin metallic with blood and fear. She catalogues her shaking hands, the sting in her scraped arm. Old habits would tell her to run, to disappear and survive however she could. Not this time.

Fear crystallizes into something harder, a stubborn ember at her core. She isn't just a bystander in Silas Carver's world. If they want a fight, she'll bleed for it—she'll make them remember her name.

Security glass gleams under the gaze of morning, honeyed sunlight diffusing through the sleek lines of Silas Carver's war room. The glass walls stand cold and silent as a tomb, muting the city's roar beyond. Electronic locks hum, sealing out the world. Monitors flicker with grainy night footage—Hana's slender figure darting through the riptide shadows of her quiet street—and a chorus of tension throbs in the air.

He strides in fast, every inch the phantom king, his suit immaculate and his jaw hard as steel. Reynolds, the grizzled chief of security, is already on his feet—shoulders squared, tablet in hand. Next to him sits Kate, pale in the sterile glow, her fingers dancing over a digital map, eyes sharp as razors behind wire frames.

"Every thread, every camera, every inbound call." Silas's words slice the air, clipped as a guillotine. "Cross-reference every threat in the last forty-eight hours—pull up every anomaly within a half-mile of Hana's block." His voice leaves no room for hesitation.

Kate's screen ignites with feeds: endless halls of pixels, faces blurred, cars creeping along curbs, a staggered outline of two men—motion stuttering as they vanish into rain-black alleys. She stabs at her keyboard. "Pattern matches two masked subjects, no exact ID. They synced device signals, likely burner comms, then faded. This wasn't amateur hour."

Silas's jaw moves just once, tension coiled beneath his skin. He doesn't sit—never does when the world stinks of threat. Reynolds murmurs a string of security enhancements, but the sound blurs, lost beneath the harsh music of his heart.

Beneath them, the city simmers—a living thing fed on secrets and power, always hungry. In Manhattan's gleaming arteries, alliances and vendettas restlessly churn. Here, every camera is a gun, and every handshake conceals a blade.

Silas reviews the threat reel. A freeze-frame captures Hana's storm-bright eyes, wide and raw beneath the electric glare. That image lodges beneath his ribs, stoking a fierce, cold anger. The war is constant, evolving—an ecosystem feeding on information and shadow. One misstep, one slip, and blood stains the floor. Not this time.

He's moving before the team can breathe relief. His shoes bite on marble tile, as pristine and unforgiving as a chessboard. The conference suite waits: wood paneling so dark it swallows the light, a sweep of city skyline aglow behind crystalline panes. Malcolm Voss stands alone—his tailored charcoal suit immaculate, gray eyes unblinking, the ghost of a sneer on his lips.

"Silas. Didn't expect you so soon," Voss starts, folding his arms.

"You've always been slow to learn." A hard smile curves Silas's mouth, cold as a winter dawn. He drops a folder onto the table—screenshots, encrypted messages, a digital paper trail crawling straight to Voss's inner circle. "Your men made Hana a warning. You'll call them off, or your media darling routine gets torn apart piece by piece. One spill, Malcolm—every network in this city will see the filth in your veins."

Malcolm tries for bravado, but sweat beads high on his collar. "You play with fire, Carver. You forget whose company you keep."

"I never forget. I bury." Silas's eyes go wolf-pale. "Touch her again. You'll need more than a lawyer."

For a heartbeat, the sound of blood rushing is louder than any threat Voss can muster. Silas leaves him floundering in his own shadow.

He doesn't rest; he never can. Digital locks blink green as he stalks back toward his domain, passing beneath low amber lights. A private call. His thumb finds the secure line, encryptions spooling out like a tangled web. Senator Salvatore appears on the wall screen, lips pursed, gaze oily and impassive.

"Senator," Silas says, voice low and lethal. "Let's not waste each other's time. My evidence shows you've been feeding hospital board directives straight into the pockets of Lucien Blackwell's enemies and lining your own along the way."

"You have nothing admissible," Salvatore snaps.

"Not in court, perhaps. But the Fourth Estate hungers for scandal." Silas flicks over files—ledgers, voice snippets, names inked in the currency of ruin. "You'll call off your dogs. Or every channel, every feed, will burn with the truth by morning."

The senator's jaw flexes; silence blooms in the space between threats.

Later, night coats the office in indigo glass. Silas stands before the map—red blips multiplying where enemies converge. Kate stands by, watching as he orders sweeping data drops, message encryptions, counter-surveillance. Reynolds assigns teams in clipped code, agents fanning out to shadow Hana's every breath. Orders ripple in practice d efficiency—his empire, built for war.

Across Manhattan's fractured circuits, another battle begins. Leaks tumble into the city's veins. Voss's empire sags under the first lash, Salvatore's phones melt with frantic calls. The world outside will wake to scandal, panic, run.

Silas ends the final call and stands, spine a steel rod, palms pressed to the cold glass. The city beats its secrets beneath him—gold and blue and midnight. His reflection stares back, hollow-eyed, jaw knotted, but another emotion flickers there: dread and a grit too savage to break. He will not let them touch her. He cannot.

Behind the glass, the war hums, endless and unseen. Silas Carver watches the city flicker—and makes himself a promise, cold as the blade in his hand: none of them, not Victor Kane, not Senator Salvatore, not Malcolm Voss, will ever cut this close again. Not while he still breathes.

The safe house breathes with silence, thick and clinical, its bare concrete walls absorbing every sound. Fluorescent lights hum, flickering as if warning of something half-seen. Silas steps through the threshold, the door's steel weight groaning shut behind him, and scans the room—cramped, windowless, filled with the uneasy scent of bleach and old coffee grounds. Hana sits hunched in a battered armchair. Her legs are drawn to her chest; her knuckles, mottled from gripping the fabric, press against her mouth. Her face is ghost-pale, but those eyes of hers—sharp, dark, relentless—meet his with a question as old as fear. He nods once, but the truth folds itself around the room: they cannot call this place safe.

"Are we actually secure here?" Her voice is raw, scraped by panic and defiance.

"No one who means you harm can step through that door," Silas replies, careful to keep the rough edge from his words, though he knows even steel can be bent by enough force—or enough desperation. He hangs his coat, aware of the gun holstered at his side, and sits opposite her at the battered kitchen table. Hana's hands tremble in the harsh gleam of LED overheads. Shadows cling to the lines of her face; the grit of the city still streaks her torn sleeve, and blood beads where her arm met rough metal behind the bodega.

She places the white envelope between them, flipping it so the block letters glare up like a wound. Silas sits with his hands pressed together, jaw clamped, as she picks through her memory of the alley: "I heard them before I saw them. Boots, two sets. I didn't think they'd—" Her breath snags. "They knew exactly what to say. 'Stay quiet. Tell Silas we are watching.' Just like that. They grabbed me, I got free, but they could've—" She shakes her head and looks away.

Silas, usually a fortress, finds the old control rotting inside him, plucked raw by the sight of her shaking. Underneath rage, guilt coils tight. He forced her into this world—with its shadows, its scars, its enemies. Kane's power shifts in the city's darkness, Selena Voss's crooning voice hisses alliance with monsters, and every enemy seems to have her scent now. He'd made a promise to be her protector, but protection has sharp edges—edges that wound her even as he tries to wield them.

His voice emerges, sandpapered and low. "If I could pull you out of this, I would." He leans in, searching her gaze. "But every path out draws blood. I won't—can't—let them touch you." His confession isn't comfort, but it's the shape of his truth, heavy and helpless on the table between them.

She bristles, the fire in her breaking through. "I'm not running. You don't own my fear." For a moment, Hana is all will. Even as her body shakes, the words become armor. "I know what danger is, Silas. I've spent most of my life outrunning it." She fixes him with a glare that stings of salt and pride. "I'm not your secret to hide."

His hand finds the envelope, smoothing the paper as if he could erase the threat inside. He wants to promise her sunlight and safety, but the world outside is run by men and women drunk on secrets. Victor Kane waits for a misstep, Damian Locke feeds on the Brotherhood's weakness, and Selena's operatives dig at every crack. Silas built an empire to control such threats, but none of his algorithms or blackmail files shield against this—this bare, human terror.

Sirens wail somewhere beyond the steel door, their song a distant brush with ordinary life. Before the sound can fade, a brittle shatter splits the room. Glass rains inward from the rear, fragments shimmering in air heavy with electric dread. Masked figures, faces blurred beneath layers of black, barrel through—the echo of Kane's tactics, Selena's ruthlessness etched in silhouette.

Instinct takes Silas. He seizes Hana's wrist—her skin so small and breakable under his grip—and drags her behind an overturned sofa. The acrid scent of cordite erupts as Silas fires, bullets cracking through plaster and panic alike. Hana fumbles with one hand, phone shaking as she stabs the emergency code into the keypad. The world contracts to animal senses: the thunder of blood, the grit of splinters biting into knees, the metallic sting of her hair against his jaw as he bends to cover her.

A figure lurches through the kitchen, knife gleaming. Silas shoots, the intruder's curse dissolving into the chaos. Another crashes back through the window as Hana's call connects, her voice taut and urgent—"We're under attack, safe house twelve, now, now, now—" Their world narrows to bright pain and movement. In seconds that feel like a lifetime, the assailants scatter, one trailing blood, another cursing in a language that slithers with threats.

Stillness seeps back, broken glass crunched under trembling limbs. Silas gathers Hana, pressing her to the floor behind the torn sofa. Their bodies quake, sweat slick on their skin. His forehead thuds against hers; his breath is a trembling vow against her cheek.

"They will have to burn this city to ash before they lay a hand on you," he whispers, voice shaking with a promise deadlier than any enemy's threat.

She closes her eyes, voice rough as gravel but certain. "I believe you, Silas. Even if I'm afraid."

Nothing left but the sound of their breath and the sirens closing. Silas drags the battered couch against what's left of the door. He sits beside Hana, shivers still rippling through him. They cling together—blood, fear, and shattered resolve between them—knowing the night is far from over.

Choosing Love

Silas leads Hana through the penthouse's labyrinth of silent halls, the aftermath of the city's chaos breathing somewhere below, all sound and violence trapped on the other side of glass and steel. There's a hush to this hour, a tension that seeps into the bones. The secluded sitting room, tucked into the farthest reaches of his domain, feels untouched by the world's threats—a sanctuary of stone and glass, lunar light draped over midnight velvet and pale wood. He closes the door with a soft click, an ancient gesture that declares: here, the world cannot touch us.

Moonlight breaks across the room in oblique bars, bathing one corner in ghostly silver. Silas walks to it and sits, where shadows mimic roses on the wall, their petals tumbling in secret patterns. He gestures for Hana to take the other chair, upholstered in indigo so dark it threatens to swallow the light. Between them, a low table gleams like water, scattered with a single white petal—an orphan from an earlier bouquet, forgotten but betraying presence. Out in the night,

Manhattan glitters. Here, everything is pared down to heartbeat and b
reath.

For a moment, neither speaks. The city's pulse is dimmed, their shared silence dense as velvet. When Silas finally lifts his gaze to hers, something in his face looks stripped bare—like winter branches after a storm.

"If I lost you," he says, and the edge in his voice doesn't mask the fracture underneath, "it wouldn't just be losing someone. It would be losing a part of myself I never believed still existed."

His hands rest on his knees, white-knuckled though he tries to hide it. "I never thought there was anyone who could tear through the walls I've built. I told myself no one would ever get behind them again."

Silas's words hang unfinished in the air, sharp as glass. The gold in his eyes flickers with the city's reflected fire.

He stands suddenly, as if the need to move overrides his endless discipline. Crossing to the massive windows, he places both hands against the glass. The city below sprawls, a hive of power and danger, the distant hum of sirens drifting up like an uneasy prayer. Out there, Victor Kane's shadow prowls through newsrooms and back alleys, Selena Voss and Damian Locke weaving their schemes in the substructure of New York's dark heart. But here, the world reduces to two people, the galaxy of his empire receding before a single reckoning.

He's still for so long that Hana wonders if he'll speak again. But then, without turning, his voice softens—thinner and more human than reputation would admit. "You grounded me, Hana. When everything burned—when enemies circled and I didn't know which lines to sever or which to defend—somehow, you made me remember I was still a man. Not just a strategist. Not just the shadow everybody else talks about. You made me believe I hadn't been turned completely to stone."

His words tremble at the last, a war between sentiment and all the armor he's learned to wear. The city glows in the planes and hollows of his face, while his reflection in the glass is disrupted by streaks of distant lightning.

Once, years ago, Silas watched his mother die beneath that same urban sky. Since then, every room he's filled has been a fortress: elegant, impenetrable, scripted to keep loss from ever finding its way back inside. That childhood vow—never let anyone close enough to wound you—has shaped him. Every mission for the Brotherhood, every calculated risk, every inscrutable answer in the press. Even now, with threats multiplying outside and betrayal tightening around the Brotherhood's throat, he clings to the illusion of unshakeable control.

But control is a myth in this moment. He hears it in the ragged edge of his breathing, feels it in the question he's never dared to ask aloud: What is left if Hana walks away? Victor's attacks, Selena's promises of ruin, even the specter of the Brotherhood's own secrets—they threaten from the outside. Inside, the fear is colder, more honest: that loving someone is the greatest risk, and that to grasp at hope is to gamble the last piece of yourself.

Behind him, Hana sits quietly. Her arms, which at first were folded protectively, begin to loosen; her eyes search for fault lines in the lines of his shoulders, the telltale tension that reveals just how much this costs him. The echo of last night's violence lingers in her posture, but now it is overtaken by something else—a slow, dawning recognition. Beneath the myth, Silas Carver is simply a man afraid of loss, desperate to protect the one thing he never planned on needing.

The hush in the room deepens, heavy with all that lies unsaid. Silas turns from the window, the city blazing in his eyes. For a moment, he lets her in—all the way in. Neither moves. Words have run thin; what remains is raw, electric.

Between them, the night holds its breath.

Hana sits perched on the edge of the velvet settee, the midnight city unfurling beyond impossibly high windows. Manhattan's lights pulse, distant constellations rising and falling against the hush of a sleepless world. The air smells faintly of bergamot and expensive paper—a subtle contradiction, clean and sharp, like the penthouse itself. Under her hand, the settee's velvety nap is cool and soft, grounding her in a place that should feel untouchable, yet tonight feels oddly intimate, as if the room has closed its borders and left only the two of them to drift in its quiet orbit.

She watches the city, her heart drumming out messages she's never put into words. For a moment, her thoughts flutter back to the café: hands shaking over chipped mugs, the clang of plates, Silas's eyes that saw through her practiced smiles. She remembers the first night she met him, how his presence unsettled the space—the scent of dark roast coffee twisting with the perfume of danger, his searching gaze pinning her in place. She'd braced for judgment, expecting just another powerful man's cold indifference. Instead, he'd watched her defend herself, jaw clenched, not interceding until it mattered. She remembers how hot shame and old anger burned under her skin then, recalling other times—other men—who watched but never cared.

She thinks of betrayal: a friend who whispered her secrets into someone else's phone for a handful of cash, an ex who left her guilt-ridden and bankrupt, trust leaking from her bones one painful drop at a time. Even the small betrayals—the ones that wear a body down over years—echo in the walls tonight: empty promises, kindness with strings, the slow hardening of the heart into something armored and brittle.

Yet layered through those memories, bright as a thread of gold, there are the rare moments she let help in. When Seraphina pressed a warm scone into her hand during a rainstorm, no expectations hidden in the sugar. When Amara reminded her, quietly, that courage wasn't about standing alone but knowing when to accept a hand. The memory of Silas's voice—rich, careful, fiercely honest—reminding her she didn't have to do everything herself. Those moments pressed against the pain and proved something could endure beneath the scars.

Her gaze slides from the city to Silas, who waits by the window, the city's sodium light glazing the harsh cut of his jaw, turning his scar silver. He looks like he belongs more to the dark than the light—there's nothing soft in the set line of his shoulders, nothing careless in the care he's taken to keep his distance. But his eyes find her, searching, his guard both fully present and impossibly fragile in this room ringed with shadows.

"Silas," she says, her voice quiet but steady. "You think I don't know what it means to live with darkness? To carry it until it seeps into everything, until you start to believe you are the shadows and not the light?" She shifts, unwinding her arms from their folded defense. "If I love you...I have to love the whole of you. Not just the parts you show in flashes. That's the truth, isn't it? Real love isn't just about the easy pieces."

He doesn't move, but something in his breath changes, a wary animal poised between flight and surrender.

"You see every ugly part of me," Silas answers, voice low. "And still, you stay?"

She swallows, memory prickling in her chest. "I used to think that accepting help made me weak. That if I relied on anyone, even for a second, they'd use it against me." Her hand balls into a fist, relaxing just as quickly, the velvet imprinting into her palm. "But it never mattered how careful I was. The world found ways to break through. I can't keep pretending none of it touched me, and I can't keep hiding from what I want."

Hana rises, careful but sure, closing the distance until the moonlight spills over both of them and the city becomes nothing more than an uncertain hum behind the glass. She lifts her chin, eyes fixed on his.

"I want it all, Silas. Even the parts that hurt to look at. Even the danger that comes with your name." The urge to flee, the voice that always told her to run, to choose solitude over heartbreak—it's quieter now, almost drowned out by the thrum of hope. "If I have to risk everything to have something real, I will. I'm not running anymore."

He lets out a slow breath—a single exhale that seems to loosen an ancient grief in him. The tension between them hangs, electric, a live wire strung between what they were and what they might risk becoming. Neither moves, and yet the whole room tilts, as if balancing on a fault line. This—this is the threshold.

She crosses it. Hana reaches for his hand. Their fingers meet, tentative, her skin warm against his cool steadiness, and the contact is enough to shrink the vast, lonely room until it feels like safety. For one fragile heartbeat, everything dangerous fades beyond the windows. Here, with hands clasped and hearts thudding, no enemy—not even Victor Kane or his coalition of rival predators—can break the fragile sanctuary they are about to choose.

Moonlight brushes the penthouse walls with cool silver, pooling around Hana's form nestled on a velvet settee, and glinting off the skyscraper windows behind Silas. The city beyond is a living constellation—windows blinking, a helicopter slicing the dark, sirens a faint electric hum. Inside, the hush hangs, dense as velvet. Silas stands motionless at first, etched against glass, shoulders rigid beneath the trim of his white shirt. Hana sits across, but the space between them feels charged—tugging, magnetic, as if every shadow in Manhattan has gathered to witness this hour.

He watches her. There's a tremor in the way her lips part, the scrape of her palm against her jeans. Her eyes flick, uncertain, but refuse to fall away from his. Silas steps forward, his careful, seamless armor finally showing hairline cracks. His breath dips shallow; every move—each step toward Hana—ripples with the ache of abandonment and the hope of reprieve.

Hana doesn't turn from his approach. Her chin rises, the faintest defiance in her gaze. She waits, pulse likely a war drum in her ears. Silas looms closer, the raw edge of need darkening his eyes, until only inches span their divide.

"I want to understand," Hana murmurs, her voice a low thread strung taut between them. "Not just the pieces you let everyone see."

He lowers himself to her level, close enough that he catches the faint trace of city air and her shampoo—a ghost of mint and something woodland, sharp and clean against the somber room. For a heartbeat, he hesitates. His hand hovers over the back of her hair. The ambient glow of the city catches the silver at his temple and the stark line of his jaw.

Silas's voice is a rasp. "If you stay, you see all of it. Not just the man you think you know." There's a pleading that slips through—naked, unguarded. "If you can't accept that…"

Her fingers wrap around the fabric at his chest, not pulling him in, not pushing him away. "I already made my choice."

Something in his restraint shatters.

Her lips lift as she surges upward, meeting his. The contact is both a clash and a release—she is trembling, but she presses closer, and he drinks in the stuttering warmth of her breath. The room contracts, soundless but for their mingled gasps and heartbeats. His hand finds the line of her jaw, slow and careful, thumb sweeping beneath her ear, holding. She melts into it, fingers knotting in his shirt until the fine cotton creases.

Silas moves with a starving kind of reverence, as though she might vanish if he lets go. She kisses back fiercely, tangling hope with desperation. Their mouths brush, part, return; his other hand cups the back of her head, anchoring her in the living present.

Neither speaks. Words are just breath now, memory of pain dissolving with each press of mouth to mouth, as if to write a new contract between them sealed in skin and salt and night air. Hana flattens her palm over his heart, feeling the rapid thunder there. He inhales shakily, holding her as if she's the last real thing in a city of ghosts.

The kiss deepens. She tastes something sharp—peppermint and the echo of whisky from before—and he tastes her fear and resolve both. Together they meet in that broken place between longing and dread.

He pulls back by slow degree, still framing her face, forehead to hers. Both breathe as if they've crossed continents, lungs not quite catching up to what has changed between them. He searches her gaze, seeking confirmation in the dilation of her pupils, the uneven smile wavering on her lips.

"We survive this together," she whispers. "Not alone. Not anymore."

"Together," he breathes, a vow scratched raw. City lights ripple through the tears unshed in his eyes.

The air inside the room grows denser, heavy with things unsaid and things forgiven. All that separates them now is the trembling hush between breaths. Silas presses his forehead against hers, grounding himself not in strategy or power but in her solidity, her willingness to stand before Manhattan's fractured beauty and claim him as her own.

Outside, twilight is seeded with danger. Silas wonders—what will Victor Kane's next move be? What subterranean currents has Selena Voss already set in motion from her perch in the halls of power? Damian Locke's name gnaws at the edge of his consciousness, a warning that fear can be harnessed or destroyed, depending on the hand that wields i t.

But for this moment, wrapped in Hana's acceptance, Silas allows himself the smallest hope. Not absolution, not the naive dreaming of fools, but something fiercer—a resolve forged by exposure and risk. She is no longer just a shield or prize or liability to be secreted away. She has become the axis on which his battered world turns, the courage he finds when strategies run dry and all that's left is the desperate, beautiful need to trust.

The night hovers outside the glass, humming with peril and possibility. Inside, Silas and Hana stand united by the wide city window, braced together—fragile, yes, but unbroken—for whatever storm the next dawn will bring.

Ashes into Roses

The strategy suite perches high above downtown, a glass fortress locked inside perpetual, rain-washed dusk. Reflections of city towers fracture across the glossy conference table; the scent of scorched espresso and ozone clings to the filtered air, thrown up by a summer thunderstorm that flickers with distant copper light. Silas Carver stands rigid at the head of the room, eyes flinty, jaw ticking as he sweeps his attention across rows of open files glowing cobalt on dark screens. Caius sits near the glass, hands gliding over his tablet, his silhouette razor-sharp, while Lucien, arms folded, flicks through legal exhibits with the patience of a man waiting for the gavel to drop. Darius's voice crackles from the wall screen, hospital badge still clipped to his collar, his gaze shadowed by sleepless resolve, and Orion spins coded glyphs across a minimalist keyboard, neon blue rippling beneath his fingers.

A barrage of forensic files—clipped voices, signatures, midnight wire transfers, memos soaked in menace—falls into line at Silas's command, each one connecting a hidden corridor: Caius's old rivals laundering bribes through shell fronts, Lucien's adversaries plotting blackmail schemes, Darius's enemies siphoning hospital funds behind time-locked password doors. The names, the numbers, the faces, all mapped in clinical blue, are ready to detonate. Silas's pulse drums steady, but sweat cools at the base of his neck. He moves with surgical calm, wrapping his voice around every order.

"We have a four-minute window for coordinated release. Caius—hold the media desk hostage. Lucien, hand off legal to the press as soon as they see the first leak. Darius, monitor hospital traffic—if Kade's proxies move, go red. Orion, you block every goddamn back door to our feeds. Understood?"

Caius tips his chin, eyes knife-sharp. "Copy. If Kane or Voss tries to counter, they'll be cut off mid-sentence."

Lucien's voice is measured, no tremor at all. "I'll have the injunctions filed by the time your evidence hits the networks."

Darius doesn't blink. "I'll station security outside main admin—let the police handle the rest."

Orion grins, teeth catching the light. "Leave the firewalls to me. They won't even make the front page of a Reddit thread."

The glass hums with distant thunder, and for a heartbeat, the city feels close. Silas presses a palm to the table's chilled surface, grounding himself. He feels the weight beneath every expertly measured motion: years of watching New York's power devour its own, the city itself a maze of mirrored lies. Corruption flows here beneath skin and skyline—from the Senate chamber's velvet hush to hospital janitors bribed with blood money, news barons silkily rebranding truths for the right price. He has spent decades feeding that machine, pruning, directing, protecting what must be protected. Tonight, he's turning the blade inward. The Brotherhood stands on the knifepoint—if he slips, legacy cracks to gray dust and rot.

Screens shift, and the operation starts.

Down on the main floor, Hana slips into the communications center under a blizzard of sodium lights. The air is sharp with coffee and nerves, cables threading the carpet and monitors blooming everywhere in real-time chaos. Her expression has changed—gone is the flickering uncertainty. She is all resolve now, lips pressed tight, eyes locked on the plan Silas crafted in restless, starlit hours. She scans the cascade of bullet points once more, then steps into the circle of cameras, the city's cold lifeblood whirring around her.

Camera lights flare. Muffled shouts echo beyond the glass. Hana's voice rings clear, steel wrapped in velvet.

"Ladies and gentlemen of New York—tonight, we turn the city's hunger for secrets toward light. For decades, networks of power hid their crimes behind reputation, wealth, and threat. Let me show you what their silence cost..."

Fingers tremble, invisible except for the fierce grip she keeps on her notes. As she names names—Victor Kane, Ava Kane, Tomas Vargo, their enabler Dr. Harper—faces flash on screens, linked to emails, wire transfers, clandestine meetings, feeds spliced together with relentless precision. "These individuals sought to weaponize private truths, to blackmail, frame, and endanger. The Brotherhood exposes these crimes now, not to shield itself, but because the city deserves more."

Reporters shift, adrenaline electric in the air. Voices start loud—"Is this revenge?", "How deep does the Brotherhood's own guilt run?"—yet Hana holds the line, answering not with practiced spin, but with facts uncoiled like hot wire.

Beside her, Silas appears—pale, composed, a storm braced behind high glass. He hears Hana's heart in every word; it tightens something old in his chest, that terror of losing everything to a single flaw, a crack in the armor. Across every screen, headlines ignite—CORRUP-

TION RING EXPOSED, KANE AND VARGO UNDER INVES-
TIGATION. Cameras catch the flinch of a felled media boss; police
frogs-march a hospital administrator past security glass, the city's filth
finally bright under neon floodlights.

On the balcony, above the modulation of press and pixel, Silas
stands next to Hana. The city below glimmers, a living lattice of hope
and suspicion. He reaches for her hand, their fingers barely touching,
comfort sparking between bruised knuckles.

"They're listening," she murmurs.

He nods, the lines beside his eyes softening. "For once, the right
way."

The barrage slows. Reporters, once lions, pause to consider: not
just accusation, but the strange relief of truth, the possibility of redemption. The room—so long a shark's den—now breathes with
something lighter.

As the evening deepens, Silas and Hana stand shoulder to shoulder, watching glass towers reflect the first sparks of rain-washed light.
Screens flicker—enemies falling, allies rallying, the city's machinery
finally creaking toward justice. For a fleeting moment, amid the hush,
victory blooms—fragile, but real.

The air in the Orion Club's inner sanctum is thick with anticipation,
and perhaps for the first time in a decade, the hush isn't from suspicion—it's from focus. The polished wood of the round table glows
amber under a ring of pendant lights, their warmth a counterpoint
to the city's evening chill seeping in through leaded glass windows.
Outside, Manhattan is a mesh of neon and dusk, but here, it's only the
four of them at first: Caius at the apex, Lucien and Darius flanking him

with set mouths, Orion perched at the edge as if barely suppressing kinetic energy. Silas is a luminous square on a secure monitor, his image blinked in from his own tower of glass and shadow, his voice silk and steel.

"Every one of you knows the game by now," Caius begins, voice as precise as a scalpel, eyes lingering pointedly on Lucien before flicking to Orion, then Darius. "But this isn't a game anymore. Today, we saw what happens when we uncover their rot. We back Silas and Hana, and we take every bit of ammunition out of Victor Kane's and Selena Voss's hands before they reload. Money, connections, influence—deploy it all. We leave nothing to chance."

Orion's fingers tap the tabletop, nails clicking soft as insect wings. "Already swept the city for chatter. Damian Locke's name keeps surfacing on the back channels. He's hungry, but we're quicker."

Darius leans forward, a tension in his shoulders—he's just come off a shift at the hospital, the ghosts of triage still lingering beneath his suit. "Financial pressure is nothing compared to what we've just blown open. Caius, you know my hands are clean, but that won't stop Harper or his watchdogs from trying to bleed us public."

Lucien, as always, says nothing until he's damn sure of every angle. When he speaks, he's already dealt the next hand. "We're not here to play defense. We're going to outflank them. I have pre-emptive counter-suits and affidavits ready. They want to drag our names through mud? They'll drown in it first." He snaps his battered briefcase open. The scent of worn leather and expensive paper cuts through the room as he lays out files—some crisp, some dog-eared from months of clandestine war. "Court dates are stacking up. We protect our own. Nobody gets left out, not this time."

Darius shifts, offering a tablet. On its screen, Lila's face flickers in from the hospital security office. Her hair is pulled back, eyes clear but rimmed red from battle. "We just finished staff interviews. Surveillance footage is patched to you now. Two board members colluded with Locke's crew and Harper's backroom. NYPD has them in custody." Behind her, a uniformed officer hauls a suited man past the camera; the moment is freighted, electric.

"Good work, Lila," says Orion, his voice softer, some of the glibness replaced by real gravity.

Orion clears his throat and swivels a monitor toward the table. "Firewall's live. Whatever Kane's freaks threw at us—fake footage, hacked comms—it's all locked out. I'm restoring every compromised account, plugging leaks, erasing footprints." Bright code scrolls across the screens: glowing armor.

Caius—who once would've scorned tech, trusting only in cold numbers and colder resolve—nods. "Keep it watertight, Orion. No repeat of the London debacle."

A flicker of humor sparks in Orion's eyes, quickly doused by the seriousness of the hour. "Only if Lucien promises not to sue me for hacking my own accounts."

Lucien huffs, amusement a rare fracture in his controlled mask. "I'll think about it. After we torch Kane's empire."

A hush falls. Even banter is fraught, colored with gratitude and exhaustion. Somewhere behind them, Amara, Seraphina, and Elara stand—each woman an anchor, their presence silent but solid, the gravity that keeps the Brotherhood's orbit from collapsing.

On screen, Silas's features are shadowed, rain slipping down the glass behind him. His gaze sweeps the table—brothers who were once rivals, now tempered by a savage loyalty. The lines around his mouth soften. He knows too well the cost of fractured trust: the missed signals, open wounds healed over by necessity, old betrayals that never quite vanish. Yet tonight the war room hums with an uneasy but unmistakable unity.

Silas's eyes linger on the edge of the room, to Hana somewhere just out of frame—not merely a civilian, not some fragile guest. She's become a center of gravity as well, the reason lines have been crossed and old debts summoned.

They raise their glasses—some crystal, some battered metal flasks. There are no toasts, only the sound of glass and steel colliding, low and defiantly alive. Their hands are steady, their voices quiet, the silence rich with everything not spoken: forgiveness, fear, hope, the will to burn the city's secrets for a future none could have imagined alone. It's enough. For now. The Brotherhood stands, reforged.

Night leans against the glass bones of Silas's penthouse, the city draped beneath in molten ribbons—headlights snaking through avenues, Times Square pulsing with fractal rainbows, the sky bleeding lavender behind spires of light. The hush inside is absolute, broken only by the whisper of air through living green. Silas's garden, cultivated with monastic precision at this impossible height, shivers with a life all its own: citrus leaves gleaming, orchids echoing color into the gloom, a symphony of growing things pushing against the cold edge of steel and g lass.

Silas leads Hana forward, the world of headlines, betrayal, and public reckoning left behind, if only for these brief moments. Shadows catch the silver in his hair, exhaustion etched into the set of his jaw, but resolve anchors his movements. In his hands, a bouquet: petals flaming scarlet into apricot, golden edges bleeding pink and lavender, the perfume intoxicating—earthy, sweet, sun-warm even in this cocoon of midnight and skyscraper hush. These are nothing like the blackened roses of their first tangled nights; there is no message of warning here, only a challenge: bloom, despite everything.

He says nothing at first. He offers the blooms with a gaze whose gray depths churn with words unspoken—a truce, a promise, a silent invocation that defies the world outside these windows.

Hana takes the roses. Her fingers tremble, almost imperceptibly, as she traces along the unfurling edges of each petal, feeling the tiny scars and velvet softness in turn. Light from the city dips into the vase, catches on raindrop crystals that ornament the leaves, turning the bouquet liquid and unreal. She can't help but inhale, the scent grounding her somewhere elemental, far away from cameras and doubt.

"You didn't have to," she whispers, her voice thin but alive, woven with awe. "After everything..."

His answer is quiet, raw. "Maybe I did." He brushes a loosened strand of her hair behind her ear, and in that gesture, there's an apology and a question—will you stay? Can this become real?

She looks at him, really looks, the way she'd once studied the faded scar above her own brow in the mirror—testing the truth of her reflection. In the lines around Silas's mouth, in the fine shudder of breath he steadies before her, she reads the toll the day has taken. Their enemies—the ruthless Victor Kane, cold intellect shining from his predatory eyes, Selena Voss dealing in secrets and sabotage, Damian Locke's shadow prowling still in the city's digital veins—press relentlessly at the edges of this peace. The world they stand in was hard-won, and she feels its cost with every heartbeat.

She holds the stems tighter and, for just a moment, the old urge to shrink away, to guard her heart with sharp laughter and silence, flares.

Yet the petals in her hands are real and alive. What would it mean to accept something so bright in the aftermath of scorched earth?

He draws her in, hands settling at her waist, steady as gravity. "Hana." The way he says her name—soft, immutable—erases miles of distance.

She lets herself rest against him, fitting her cheek to his chest, feeling the slow, uncertain pulse beneath expensive fabric. His fingers graze her back, her hair, and he presses his lips to her temple.

"We're not those people anymore," he says. "You and I. After everything—after today—starting again isn't just possible. It's necessary. I don't want to wear silence as armor. I want..." His voice falters, catching emotion sharper than any blade, "I want us. Together. No more secrets."

Her shoulders sag with relief, the long coil of vigilance inside her finally loosening. All those years spent believing vulnerability meant exposure, weakness—tonight, the old logic flickers, shatters. The crucible of public battle, of dirt dragged into light, has forged some new alloy within her. She thinks of the look on Silas's face when she stepped in front of the world's cameras, the way his steely calm broke when her words cut through the narrative the antagonists had spun like webbing. She found strength in the fire. She knows he did, too.

"I was so afraid letting you close would break me," she murmurs. "Turns out, it was the only way I could breathe again."

He studies her, every line of his body taut with the tension of confession. "I should've told you everything sooner," he admits. "But I was afraid. Of losing this. Of losing you."

She laughs, not to dismiss, but to mark the moment—light, effervescent. "I guess we're both scared," she says. "But what comes next is ours to write."

He kisses her—slow, reverent, as if learning the contours of forgiveness. The garden holds them, cocooned in humid green and golden lamplight.

"Whatever storm comes," he says—this time unbreakable—"as long as you're here, I'm ready."

They stand wrapped in each other's arms, city lights tumbling at their feet, the bouquet vivid between them. Against the canvas of midnight, the roses blaze—faithful proof that even after ashes, color erupts, and hope has roots. As Silas and Hana turn, side by side, to meet whatever trembles on the horizon, the garden flickers around them and the future—no longer a thing to fear—sprawls wide and wild ahead.

The Hidden Flame

Glass shards glint beneath the city's midnight glow, scattered like warning stars across Silas Carver's penthouse floor. The roses—black, red, ruined—spill their faded petals between leather-bound tomes knocked from shelves in the battle that cracked both silence and pride. Above it all, the thrum of nocturnal New York dims to a low hum behind the paneled windows, as if the world itself pauses to draw breath.

Silas sits on the velvet sofa, his back against the cool curve, the line of his jaw shadowed and motionless. Hana's weight eases into his side. Her cheek brushes his shoulder, uncertain at first, as though she expects him to turn away, to reassemble that mask built for boardrooms and war rooms. Instead, Silas waits, his posture unyielding save for the hand—knuckles grazed and ring finger trembling ever so slightly—resting inches from hers.

She closes her eyes, letting the hush settle between them.

"I still remember," Hana murmurs, so softly that uncertainty stains every syllable. "You—sitting in the corner of that café. Just... watching." She huffs a laugh, brittle as frost. "I thought you hated me. Or that you were cataloguing my faults for tomorrow's headlines."

Silas doesn't move, not yet. The roses could have been his sigil: love and violence, their scent curling through memory with a bittersweet charge that never fades. Petals scatter close to Hana's bare foot, damp where wine seeped into the rug and blossom.

"You didn't deserve it," Hana whispers. She names what followed as if enacting a ritual, her voice edged like glass. "My mother's leaving. My father's debts. That night when Mark found me—" Her throat flares with color. "I thought I'd never get out. I thought every hand that reached for me just wanted to pull me down farther—" Words collapse into tremulous silence.

Her breath stirs the scent of crushed petals. She leans harder, as if seeking warmth from the only fire left unburnt.

Silas meets her gaze at last, his eyes silver and unreadable, fixed on something beyond her. Only then does the fissure at his temple soften. He reaches, not for the face that's brave enough to meet ruin, but for the memory that lingers between them.

"My mother died here," he says, quiet as fog drifting through closed streets. "I was twelve." The admission slices through shadow, a rare offering. "She left me a rose—there, on my father's desk. Black on the outside, red at the heart. Like a warning. Or a promise."

He studies the cuts scattered across his knuckles, the pain a faint echo of old wounds. "The Brotherhood—they gave me purpose. But every secret I kept for them carved something out of me. Sometimes I thought I would vanish—smoke and ash before anyone noticed what was missing."

A silence heavy enough to drown in. Then, Hana shifts, the movement scattering glass like unfinished truths. She takes his hand, brushing her thumb over the jagged line that crosses his skin. Her palm is rough, fingertips callused from plates, books, and doors slammed in self-defense—yet she holds him as if touch alone might shelter what's lef t.

"I trust you." She says it without armor, the words offered instead of demanded. Her eyes, raw and bright, are proof she means it. "I never wanted to. But I do. I can't keep fighting you and myself."

Silas's hand tightens, skin ghosting hers, as if he can trap this fragile allegiance before it flickers out. His breath skims her hair, his mouth nearer than safety. "You are... the only light left in all of this. You know that, don't you?" There's nothing strategic about the ache in his voice. "It frightens me—how much I want to keep you here."

Under the bruised lamplight, their world narrows. Silas lifts his hand, brushing his thumb below Hana's chin. The gesture is uncertain, gentle; a truce, not a conquest. She tilts her head so his fingers touch just beneath her jaw, the warmth steady and anchoring.

"You don't have to—" she starts, but Silas stops her with a look, haunted and hungry.

He closes the distance. The kiss is slow, drawn-out, and fragile. Outside, the city erupts in gold and electric white, the glow streaking across faces damp with memory. Wine and roses mingle with the aftertaste of fear, all of it fading as lips search for forgiveness they never thought to deserve.

When the world exhales again, Hana folds herself into Silas's side. She tugs the worn blanket from the back of the sofa, nestling beneath its weight until the only movement is the rise and fall of breath, shared. Silas pulls her closer, drawing the fabric over their tangled legs. Somewhere, gentle music leaks from hidden speakers; strings, distant, reminding them they are still alive and still here, even if the pieces are scattered.

The penthouse settles into quiet ruin. With Hana's head on Silas's chest, her heartbeat unshielded for the first time in years, she wonders if every broken thing must always stay broken. Warmth bleeds where she once held herself cold, and as his thumb circles her scar, her story begins to rewrite itself—not with fear, but with hard-won hope. The city leans against the glass, vast and unknowable. For tonight, that's enough.

The Orion Club's hidden lounge hums with tension, a hush stretched thin across the vaulted silence. Along the paneled walls, shelves sag with battered tomes: histories, treaties, a clutch of conspiracy pamphlets bound in cracked leather. Soundproofing panels swallow the city's chaos, leaving behind the stilled hush of collective dread. Pools of warm lamplight push shadows into the corners. Footsteps crunch softly on patterned rugs as Silas Carver steps inside, the last to arrive.

Caius stands rigid near the table, jaw drawn tight, suit jacket barely hiding his restless hands. Lucien broods in an antique wingback, tapping an unlit cigar against his knee—a habit from law school, never quite lost. Darius leans into a beam of amber light, his fingers laced tight as if to wring comfort from the ghosts of old oaths. Orion paces near the drinks tray, his boots tracing the same impatient circuit.

Seraphine, ever watchful, perches at Caius's side, her hair catching the lamplight in motes of copper. Amara glides between chairs with a service so unobtrusive it borders on ritual, pouring fragrant tea—steam curls, bittersweet, cardamom, and honey—into mugs for Elara and Hana. Elara's steady gaze anchors the room. Hana arrives at Silas's side, careful, her movements precise and composed—her guard up, but the tremor in her hands betrays exhaustion's wear.

There's a quiet ballet among the women: Amara's palm resting for an extra heartbeat on Hana's shoulder, Seraphine's thumb sweeping slow over Caius's knuckles, Elara's soft nod toward Darius before handing him his cup. It's in these gestures—small, gentle, unseen by those who seek thunder in unity—that a fragile trust cements itself. A new order is being made, not in words, but in invisible lines threaded between loyalty and fear.

Caius is the first to break the silence, his voice clipped as a blade. "Victor Kane's syndicate—he's at it again." The name slashes the stillness. "Editorials, networks, rumors about... us, about you, Silas. Flooding feeds before fact, warping every story to suit his agenda. Our history, rewritten."

Lucien's eyes narrow, waxen under the lamplight. "Media's only the tip. Kane's pulled strings—subpoenas have been filed. Demand for financial records, internal correspondence... They're bayonetting our assets one by one. Legal, jurisdictional. It's dirty and it's spreading."

From the sofa, Darius exchanges a glance with Lila. He speaks, his voice deep but worn. "There's talk again at the hospital. They're reopening the probe. Patients who've never complained, now their records are red-flagged. Backed by a source none of the staff will name. Lila's position might be next—she got another anonymous warning, a threat if she doesn't help bury evidence."

Orion snorts, shaking off the heavy quiet. "Digital front's just as ugly. Our firewalls have been hammered twenty-seven times in two days. Same signature as last year's breach—the one traced back to Selena Voss's fixer. My new launch is being savaged in bot attacks, fake reviews. Someone's paying well for chaos." He flashes a jagged grin, but it doesn't reach his eyes.

Hana tenses beside Silas, her shoulders drawn up as if to ward off memory's cold. She glances at Amara, and in that look, Silas senses the stubborn, battered solidarity of survivors. He's struck by how these women, strangers months ago, forge a network of silent strength between them, holding space, refusing to let the men drown alone. For a heartbeat, the heaviness in his chest breaks—the flicker of hope smolders amid the fear.

Silas rests a nondescript folder across his lap, his wrists so tight they tremble, but he makes no move to speak. The folder's weight is more than paper—the future, compressed to a dozen secrets, tick-tocking through him like a live grenade. Around him, the others shift, sensing the fissure: his silence, the gravity of a promise unfulfilled. The club is quieter for his restraint; a hush heavier than indictment.

Caius fixes him with an unreadable stare. "There's a cost in every alliance, Silas. We all know it." He lifts his tumbler—a slow-motion toast to bridges unburned, to trust that may yet falter. One by one, hands follow: wine, scotch, tea, water—they clink, soft but certain.

The room is unified, but not unwounded. Each glance over glass, each knuckle grazed against another's skin, is a vow—unspoken, and therefore binding. Trust, here, is an if: conditional, raw, haunted by the names Kane and Voss and Locke. In the lamplight, their eyes glint with exhaustion and what might, on another night, be hope.

Rain streaks the floor-to-ceiling windows of the boardroom, city lights fractured into trembling lines of gold and red. The penthouse above thrums with distant sirens and the low metallic drone of traffic. At the dark walnut table, Silas lays the tablet—its grey screen pulsing with a silent warning—at the heart of the Brotherhood's small circle. Each man sits rigid, the hush in the room drawing oxygen from the air.

A single tap. The screen stutters, then blooms with the grainy faces of the enemy: shadows behind digital veils. The audio distorts, crackling with the guttural resonance of Damian Locke, his voice masking the blurred silhouette beside him. "This is not a declaration. It's an instruction. Media heads will receive the leaks by midnight. Your lawyers will face the first round of subpoenas tomorrow. The hospital's records…" The video warps—just a flicker, but enough for Lucien's mouth to tense. "…will not remain untouched. You were legends. Now, you'll be lessons."

A faint trace of cigar smoke seems to rise from the screen—phantom, imagined, perhaps, but lingering in the tense, acid silence swallowing the boardroom.

Caius moves first, his hands steady as he pages through a set of files that accompany the video. "Locke didn't write these. See the language in clause twenty-three? That's Victor Kane's lawyer. They're not acting alone." He flips a folder, and the sharp snap echoes off the glass. "Every signature on this coalition—I recognize most. Old London funds. Russian holding companies. Selena Voss isn't just pulling political strings; she's financing this, and she's not hiding it."

Darius's phone vibrates. He turns, eyes sharp as scalpels, and steps into the glass-walled alcove. Low words into the receiver—pauses, reassurances that barely mask dread—float back as he returns. "Lila's supervisor found the ER records accessed. There's a threat, specific, against her credentials. If she doesn't walk, she'll lose her license or worse." His jaw flexes, fighting something too raw for words.

Lucien leans over the tablet, scrolling quickly, his gaze sharpening on a clutch of PDFs. "They're freezing our accounts—see here? Kane and Locke filed five suits in three states. Shielded by proxies, but the pattern's obvious. They want us blind and paralyzed by morning."

Across the table, Orion's fingers dart over his matte-black laptop, the tap-tap-tap punctuating the swirl of fear drifting across the city skyline beyond. His eyes flick, first anxious, then predatory. "This isn't script-kiddie stuff. This IP—dammit—shows up in the code we flagged last winter, the hospital ransomware. It's all being run out of one backend. We're not looking at copycats. This is orchestration. Kane, Locke, Voss—they've stopped competing. It's a syndicate." He runs a trembling hand through his hair, knuckles pale against dark ink.

Caius glares at the streaming tablet as the screen splinters into static. "Victor Kane was always bold, but uniting with Selena Voss and Locke? That's madness. With her connections in Washington, every firewall you build, Orion, might buy us minutes, not hours."

"She'll weaponize the media, and not just mine," Silas says, his voice low enough to nearly disappear beneath the thrum of the rain. "She wants to choke truth with spectacle. The headlines will bleed us out faster than lawsuits." The words feel foreign—bitter coins held too long between molars. He studies their faces and wonders which of them will lose first.

"What if we just—move assets? Hide them offshore—" Orion starts, his tone brash but flickering.

"It won't matter, not with legal blockades in place. They'd follow every path." Lucien's calm is a razor's edge, and beneath it, a tremor of helplessness.

"Silas, you built this empire on secrets. What if they're betting you've got more to lose than anyone?" Darius's voice is quiet but loaded, a surgeon's warning before an incision.

Silas looks down at the device, the glow from its screen sickly on his fingers. The specter of his mother's death edges the memory, that feeling—suffocating helplessness as the world spun outside his control. He wants to shield them, all of them, yet his own strength is a fortress crumbling beneath floodwater. Every avenue—media, law, medicine, tech—has become a field sown with mines. If one blows, none walk away unscarred.

Beyond these walls, the world is turning: headlines drafted by invisible hands; legal threats that move like chess pieces through a shadow court; a hospital system where a click wipes out a life's work. New York's veins pulse with power, and every circuit, every archive, every whispered threat on a burner phone—they're all turning inward, strangling the very protections the Brotherhood built.

He wonders, as Damian Locke's laughter echoes through the tablet and the room falls still, how long he can keep them all afloat. There's a loneliness in command that no alliances can mend, a dark place beneath the marble and steel. Tonight, he faces it square-on: not as the strategist in the shadows, but as a man bracing against the storm he always feared might come.

Silas closes the tablet. In the sharp silence, the future feels as thin and fragile as glass. The Brotherhood is besieged, and every ghost they've ever made has learned to work together.

Dusk spills into night at the edge of the Orion Club's rooftop garden, the hum of New York stretching away beneath a sky turning iron-grey. Silas stands at the stone balustrade, the wind teasing his collar, Hana's hand warm in his. She slides her fingers between his with quiet certainty, palm pressed to palm, as if anchoring them both against the current of the world. Around them, the Brotherhood gathers—Caius's sharp gaze trained on the horizon, Lucien leaning back with arms crossed, Darius and Orion shoulder to shoulder, their partners close, a web of alliances remade in trust and necessity.

Soft light glimmers from brass lanterns scattered among rose bushes trailing scarlet petals and silver dew. The earth smells rained-on and raw, city smoke blending with lavender and a faint hint of ozone. Hana's hair, tousled from the wind, brushes her cheek. The city thrums below, a living beast of light and shadow, sirens rising and falling in the distance. Every face on this rooftop is marked by exhaustion and defiance.

Silas lifts his chin, grey eyes catching the last flare of the sun—orange fire bleeding through thickening clouds. His voice is low, threaded with something raw and unbreakable.

"We know who hunts us," he says. "Victor Kane pushes his media knives deeper each day. Damian Locke's shadow slips through boardrooms and alleys, and Selena Voss—she'd see us razed if it filled her coffers and left her enemies bled dry." Each name lands heavy, their collective threat electric in the cold air. "But we're not finished. Not by storms, nor scandal, nor men and women who trade lives for power. Our scars don't break us. They make us sharp."

A tremor runs through Hana's frame—fear warring with pride—but she straightens, letting the hard neon edge of the city reflect in her eyes. The Brotherhood's partners gather closer, hands brushing, eyes flicking between one another in silent encouragement.

Silas squeezes her hand, and for a heartbeat, the mask he wears slips. He is a strategist who's counted costs in secrets and souls, yet tonight, a different current flows beneath his words—a courage that tastes almost like hope.

Nobody speaks. Lantern light dances over pale knuckles, over Seraphina's delicate tattoo, over Amara's crescent moon, over Elara's silver necklace trembling at her throat.

Hana breaks the hush—a clear, ringing voice that lifts above the traffic's distant thunder. "They want us to believe love is a weakness," she says, steady and clear, "that hope is a danger. But you—" she looks around, shoulders squared, "—you taught me that love builds armies. I'm done running from the past. I'd rather face every enemy out there than deny what we are. We stand together, or we don't stand at all."

Orion lets out a low whistle. Darius's lips tilt in a rare, quiet smile; Lucien nods once, slow and measured. Caius glances briefly at Seraphina, offering his hand, unspoken emotion in the set of his jaw.

The wind sharpens. Hana shivers—Silas slides closer, anchoring her against his side. Above them, the sky bruises—charcoal streaked with fleeting orange, the first fat drops of rain whispering against stone. The city below is a jigsaw of restless light—illuminated windows, blinking towers, headlights spilling along avenues like veins alive with urgent purpose.

Silas turns to face his brothers and their partners; city gloom blurs the edges of his silhouette. Wordlessly, they follow his gaze, all eyes on the storm boiling up from the west. Every trouble Kane stirs, every blow Locke and Voss threaten, feels near enough to touch.

He bends and presses a kiss to Hana's brow—gentle, a vow made flesh. Rain beads on her hair. Around them, the Brotherhood and their partners form a silent line at the balustrade. The air seems loaded, heavy with promise and with all that might yet shatter.

Silas stares into the roiling clouds over Manhattan, feeling the enormity of what lies ahead. Each trial—the betrayals, the secrets, each scarred heart—has been kindling. The fire that's about to catch will burn away all illusion, all comfort, all half-felt vows. What darkness would he weather for Hana, for these men and women at his flanks? He thinks of the cost—might be trust, love, or even a piece of his soul. Yet hope, fragile as glass, holds its steady glint. Even as the night stretches wide and perilous, love is the one truth the world cannot blacken.

The city lights flicker on, thousand-eyed and unblinking. Wind tears the scent of roses and steel through the air. As the Brotherhood faces the coming storm, no one looks back. Only forward, into dusk.

Epilogue

The war wasn't over. It had only changed shape.

Silas stood with Hana in the Brotherhood's hidden lounge, the weight of a hundred secrets pressing against the walls. Around him, Caius, Lucien, Darius, and Orion carried their scars like armor; their women stood beside them, living proof of the battles already fought.

The Brotherhood was united, but shadows lengthened with every breath. Enemies were no longer whispers—they were gathering, circling, striking from corners of finance, politics, law, and blood.

And yet, in the quiet of that moment, Silas felt something he had thought impossible.

Hope.

Hana's hand slipped into his, steady, unflinching. The black-and-red roses of his past had given way to new blooms—living, breathing, defiant against the darkness. She was the light he never expected to find, the flame he could never extinguish.

"This isn't the end," Silas whispered, his voice a vow, his gaze locked on hers.□

"It's the fire before the storm."

Outside, the city lights burned. Inside, the Brotherhood prepared for their reckoning.□

And in Silas's heart, the hidden flame roared to life.

Final Thoughts

You've walked with me through shadows and secrets, through the fire that threatened to burn love to ash. Silas Carver's story is one of silence, scars, and the terrifying beauty of vulnerability. He was the phantom who swore he would never surrender his heart—until Hana Brooks taught him that love is not weakness, but survival.

This is not the end of The Orion Brotherhood. In truth, it is the storm's gathering breath. Every scar, every betrayal, every vow whispered in the dark has led us here—to the brink of the Brotherhood's greatest reckoning.

Thank you for reading, for believing, and for stepping into this dangerous, passionate world with me. Your heart, like mine, now carries a piece of Silas and Hana's journey.

Stay close. The fire is only beginning.

With gratitude and courage,

Ck Franco

Review Request

LOVED the Orion Dynasty Book Series?

Click here to leave your review on Amazon.

Your review helps this dark billionaire romance world reach new readers who crave power, passion, and redemption.

Or type this link into your browser:
https://www.amazon.com/review/create-review?asin=B0FSSBP-KKP